D0801448

MISS PRIM

Other books by Jane Myers Perrine:

Persy and the Prince
The Mad Herringtons

MISS PRIM

•

Jane Myers Perrine

AVALON BOOKS
NEW YORK

Published by Thomas Bouregy & Co., Inc.
160 Madison Avenue, New York, NY 10016

Library of Congress Cataloging-in-Publication Data

Perrine, Jane Myers.
    Miss Prim / Jane Myers Perrine.
        p. cm.
    ISBN 0-8034-9757-1 (acid-free paper)
    1. London (England)—Fiction. I. Title.

PS3616.E79M57 2006
813'.6—dc22

                                            2005025401

PRINTED IN THE UNITED STATES OF AMERICA
ON ACID-FREE PAPER
BY HADDON CRAFTSMEN, BLOOMSBURG, PENNSYLVANIA

This book is dedicated to my dear husband George
who is and always has been my hero.

And to the memory of Colin Clark who brought
us all so much joy with his drums, with his smile,
and with his faith.

Chapter One

"**M**y life is ruined!" Lucinda—Lady Bertram—tossed down the letter she'd been reading and collapsed onto the chaise longue.

Lady Louisa Walker watched what promised to be a grand case of the vapors as her sister Lucinda pressed the back of her graceful hand against the perfection of her ivory forehead and sighed.

"Edward!" Lucinda appealed to her husband. "How can Cassie be so thoughtless! To deprive me of the company of my dearest sister in my time of need?"

But Louisa, long inured to such displays of emotion, calmly sipped her tea and nibbled on a lemon cake.

"Dearest, don't let yourself become overset," said Lady Bertram's adoring husband as he patted her on the shoulder. "Perhaps Louisa could stay here until you're stronger."

But Louisa—dressed fashionably in a morning dress with a high neck and puffed sleeves, and a becoming lace cap—was not sympathetic to the appeal in her sister's eyes or in her brother-in-law's voice. Indeed, it was difficult to feel compassion for a woman whose husband gave her whatever she wanted, and who had two healthy and handsome sons, a lovely estate in Oxford, as well as in a fashionable section in London.

"I'm sure," Louisa told her sister firmly, "that Cassandra would not ask me to attend her if it weren't important." In spite of the confidence with which she spoke, Louisa wasn't certain of this at all: Cassie was completely scatterbrained, and Cassie's husband Arnold was equally irresponsible.

Louisa put down her cup of tea and picked up the missive from the floor where Lucinda had thrown it. "She says that I must leave for Arnold's estate immediately. His father is ill, and they are urgently needed at his bedside."

Louisa searched the missive for more information, a task which presented great difficulty due to Cassandra's habit of crossing the page, underlining, and recrossing the page. "And"—Louisa began as she tried to interpret what little she could decipher—"that she just had a baby—" At Lucinda's gasp, Louisa amended, "No, no, I'm sorry. She has a baby staying with them and there is an outbreak of . . ." She turned the paper and held it so the light from the window fell on the page. "Needles? No, that can't be it. Meadows? No, no . . . measles! That's it. There is an outbreak of measles around Arnold's father's estate, and the baby . . . who is this baby?" Louisa turned the letter in search of enlightenment. "They dare not expose her to the disease. There!" She sat back in her chair.

"Well, for once Cassandra is showing some sense. But who is this baby?" asked Edward.

"Surely she would have told us if she were increasing again," Lucinda added.

"Unless, of course, she forgot, which is possible." Louisa searched the letter again. "She doesn't say who the baby is, just that she needs me there to take care of her as soon as possible. Well, darlings," she said briskly as she stood, "if I'm needed, I must be off. I'll pack this morning and leave at noon, if you will lend me a coach and driver, Edward."

"If you feel you must, of course I will."

"Oh, don't go, Louisa," Lucinda begged. "Don't forget how much little Michael and Elliot need you too!"

"They have to learn their Aunt Louisa doesn't live here all the time, that there are other nieces and nephews who depend on me also."

"I do love all my sisters and all my brothers and all their spouses!" Louisa reminded herself as she entered her suite and pulled the cord to call Boswell, her dresser.

"You know well, Boswell, how much I enjoy my life, so predictable and peaceful," she said to the dresser upon her entrance.

"Yes, my lady." Boswell nodded.

"You know how much I like to spend the season in London and the rest of the year with my family."

"Yes, my lady, but how nice that you can spend so much of your time with them. They treat you so well."

"Yes, Boswell, I love every one of them and am fortunate, but I do like to decide on my own where I should go in times of need."

"Certainly, my lady. That is the convenience of not having a husband."

At five-and-twenty, Louisa knew herself to be firmly on the shelf. She foresaw that the visitations to the homes of her six brothers and sisters to organize each household would be the pattern for the rest of her life. She anticipated that with a smile. Such a routine existence was precisely what she desired in life.

"Exactly, Boswell."

The trip from Oxford to Essex is not arduous, especially in Edward's cushioned carriage that clipped along at close to eight miles per hour. Louisa was certain that she would be at Longtrees in time to sort out the mystery of who this baby was, and why the child was there, before she sat down to a delicious meal prepared by Arnold's marvelous French chef.

Unfortunately, rain began to fall only minutes after

she and Boswell set out. While rounding a curve just past Bedford, the carriage slid on the wet surface and veered off the road. Fortunately John Coachman was able to shout a warning so Louisa and Boswell could brace themselves, but the sudden stop threw them around the interior and caused Louisa to bump her head.

"Are you all right, my lady?" asked the worried footman as he opened the door of the tilted carriage.

"We're fine, James," she answered, after ascertaining that Boswell had suffered no injury. Louisa refused to complain about the throbbing knot she could feel expanding on her forehead. "How are you and the carriage?"

"No damage to me or John, my lady, and little to the carriage," said James. "But I'll have to help take that wheel into town. The rim is broken. There's a small inn a little ways up the road where you can wait. I'm afraid you'll have to walk."

She jumped from the carriage only to land with a plop in mud. James held out his hand to steady her as she struggled to disengage her feet from the sucking muck. After Boswell struggled from the carriage, the two women hurried as quickly as the road and wind allowed toward the tiny building. The innkeeper put them in the only private parlor, and had a fire built so Louisa and Boswell could settle on chairs near it to dry out and warm up.

Louisa took off her hat and eyed it with disfavor. Formerly a jaunty green felt with dashing gold feathers, it now resembled a parrot after a bad day at sea. She tossed the soggy mass toward the fireplace, rested her ruined slippers on the hearth, then reached up to gently examine her forehead. The protuberance still hurt a great deal.

Beside her, Boswell snored loudly, and Louisa wished she could sleep as well, although she knew she wouldn't. It was hardly proper.

By the time John Coachman announced the repairs were completed, darkness had fallen. Determined to reach Arnold's estate, Louisa had the coach travel through the night. It was close to ten o'clock when the party arrived at Longtrees. Pleased to see lights still on, Louisa lifted the knocker at the same time the door opened.

"My lady!" Greeves, Arnold's butler, greeted her. "We expected you much earlier. I trust you had a pleasant journey?"

Louisa swept into the mansion. "It was very difficult." She was exhausted, chilled, and her head was throbbing. "If you'll excuse me, I'll go to my room. Please have a tray sent up."

"Yes, but, my lady—"

"I'm too tired to chat, Greeves. If you please?" she added in a tone no one ever dared argue with. Followed by Boswell, she ascended the stairs, looking down on an astonished Greeves, whose mouth opened and closed rhythmically as he waved his arms. "Will you send my trunks up when they have been unloaded?"

"Please, my lady!"

On a middle step, one of the waterlogged slippers fell apart. Louisa held on to the rail with one hand and took the offending articles from her feet with the other.

"Dispose of these, please, Boswell."

The dresser took the slippers and went back down the stairway.

"My lady," Greeves implored as he started up the steps after her. "Please."

Ignoring him in her longing for a warm bed and soft pillow, Louisa hurried up the stairs.

The apartment Louisa used on her visits was a beautifully furnished suite in the corner of the second floor, always kept ready for her whenever she visited Longtrees. She hurried there, entering the bedroom instead of going around the corner to the door to the sitting room which opened off the other hallway.

Once there, Louisa finally gave into the throbbing pain in her head. She closed her eyes and loosened her heavy braid, then shook her dark curls until they cascaded around her shoulders in waves and ringlets, even over her face. She sighed deeply with the release of that tension. Unbuttoning her fitted jacket and the top buttons of her traveling dress, Louisa eased the collar open so she could rub the nape of her neck. In an effort to relieve her aching head, she closed her eyes and massaged her temples.

"Well, well. What a delicious little morsel," said a deep male voice from the sitting room.

Louisa's eyes snapped open and she dropped her

hands. She froze when she saw a man standing in the doorway to the sitting room. He wore a shirt open halfway to his waist which displayed a broad manly chest covered with hair—such a great amount of hair! So thick, so . . . virile. She was almost overwhelmed by the masculinity that radiated from him. To see that much bare skin on a male over the age of three was a novel experience for Louisa. She was appalled at what this exhibition was doing to her equilibrium, circulation, and respiration. The sight made her so dizzy that she had to hold onto the bedpost; her blood was racing, causing a tumultuous pounding in her ears and chest.

His pale unmentionables were molded around powerful thighs and down to muscular calves, she noted.

For heaven's sake, she scolded herself, what were her eyes doing studying *that* part of his body? She forced herself to look at his face: thin but handsome in a debauched way, topped by dark, rumpled hair. His left eyebrow was lifted and a smile curved his mouth.

"Oh my," she whispered.

He had changed, that was why recognition had been so slow. When she'd seen him last, his face had been rounder and softer, his expression more open. Nonetheless, it was William. William Rathe. What was William doing in her bedchamber?

In one hand he held a snifter of brandy; in the other, a thin cigar from which rose a sensuous spiral of smoke.

He leaned against the door frame with grace and insouciance. "Did Arnold send you?"

He hadn't recognized her. Had she changed so much in eight years? Of course, with her hair over her face, he couldn't see her.

"No, Cassandra wrote to me." Her voice sounded amazingly conversational when compared to the tumult taking place in her body. She was, heaven forbid, becoming overwrought, and knew not what to do about it.

"Cassie? I wouldn't have thought it of her. I must thank her when I see her next."

His narrowed eyes surveyed her from toe to head. Aware of her disarray, she pulled her hair back and attempted to smooth it.

When he saw her face, recognition showed in his eyes. They opened a little wider, but his expression did not change. "Well, well, Louisa. What a surprise. Have you come to warm my bed?"

"Oh, for heaven's sake, William, you know I haven't." She suddenly became aware that she was barefoot and the top buttons of her dress were open. And she wore no hat! What would a man think of a woman who had just come in from outside with no hat? she wondered stupidly.

She was amazed and shocked at seeing her former fiancé . . . well, *not* her fiancé. The relationship had never gone that far, but she'd thought they would marry. William was the last, the very last man on earth she wanted to see her like this.

She didn't know what to do first. With her left hand she grabbed her hair again while she endeavored to button her dress with the right, and bent her knees in the hope her dress would cover her feet.

"And so, my dear Louisa, how are you?"

As he pushed himself off the door frame, Louisa straightened and met his gaze, looking into the thin face she'd adored years earlier, foolish chit that she'd been.

"Fine, William," she said as politely as if she'd been in a drawing room. "Odd to see you here." Odd was the completely wrong word. Terrible. Humiliating. Scandalous.

"I had long ago given up the idea that you would grace my bedroom, Louisa, but here you are."

"Your bedroom? These aren't your chambers. Cassie saves this apartment for me."

"Then, by all means stay, Louisa."

"How dare you, William," she gasped but the glitter in those onyx eyes made her believe he'd dare anything.

Confronted with the awareness that she was partially undressed and alone in a room with a man in a similar state, Louisa was faced with a situation she could not control using the rules of polite society.

She turned and fled.

Chapter Two

Louisa slammed the chamber door behind her and leaned against it, as if attempting to keep William on the other side. Her heart beat at a frightful rate, and she could not catch her breath. She jumped when she heard a voice.

"I'm sorry, my lady. I tried to tell you." Greeves stood beside her in the hall.

"Yes, Greeves." She turned toward him with an icy composure, difficult in her state of partial undress. "Why is *that* man in my room?"

"The viscount was invited for a visit by his lordship."

So he had acceded to the title, Louisa thought. "Why is he here? In my chambers?"

"Your suite is the finest guest suite, my lady. We did not realize you would be here when the viscount was

11

placed there. At the master's departure, he remained at the master's request. To take care of the baby."

"*He* is here to care for the baby? Isn't it odd that Arnold asked *him* to care for a baby?"

"I could not say, my lady. The viscount was here when the message came from his lordship's father. When he and your sister had to leave, her ladyship wrote you so there'd be a woman to take over."

"With *him* in *my* rooms, where am I to stay?" she asked as she watched a footman bring her trunk up the stairs, followed by Boswell.

"We have prepared the green chamber." Greeves led her down the hall. "We have a warm fire started and will bring you a tray with some nice hot tea and cook's lovely meat pie shortly."

Her bare feet were numb from the cold, her head still throbbed but, even worse, she was alone in the house with her old love. As exhausted as she was, Louisa's innate sense of propriety forced her to consider a problem.

"I cannot stay in residence, not alone with a single gentleman." The very thought caused Louisa to take a deep breath and clutch the open neck of her dress even more tightly. Perhaps, she thought brightening, perhaps she could use this to force William out of her chambers and out of her life again. She could recommend he move to an inn. In that case, she would not have to face him on the morrow.

"That's why we placed you near the suite of the master's aunt, Lady Woolton. She lives here now, in the same wing as the green chamber." Greeves continued down the hall and turned left.

"Thank you," Louisa stated as she entered her new suite. The footman followed, placed her trunk on the floor, and left. After Boswell closed the door, Louisa sat at the dressing table and allowed the dresser to brush her hair and braid it.

What must he think of her after so many years? She studied herself in the mirror. Her hair had been down, in curls instead of its normal tight braids. She looked tired, but that was to be expected after a day of travel. Her dress was wrinkled and she was exhausted, bothered by the throbbing of her head.

And she was barefoot. Most unladylike.

Well, she probably didn't look much different from that hoyden she'd been when she met William and thought herself in love with him. She'd allowed William to kiss her and had enjoyed it. Very much.

Why was life so unfair that William, of *all* people, would be the one to find her in such a coil? How could she have burst into *his* bedroom in such a state? She hated to face him again, and abhorred the turmoil he could still create in her.

With great effort, she turned her mind away from him. Certainly, she lectured herself, the man didn't really cause turmoil in her chest. She'd been startled, frightened. *That* was what caused such an emotional reaction. It would have happened if any man had suddenly appeared in her bedroom.

She again looked at herself in the mirror, this time to inspect the lump on her head. It hadn't become too discolored, although her forehead was shiny and a little dark. Perhaps it wouldn't look horrible.

A delicious morsel he'd called her when he thought she was another type of woman altogether. She must not have looked too terrible.

Drat, she cursed. Why did the man keep intruding in her thoughts? Hadn't she forgotten about him years ago, replaced him with her busy life and her family?

What was he doing now? Was he married? Certainly so. After all, he was thirty. Where was his wife?

The look she'd seen in his eyes seconds before he realized who she was, was one she'd not seen in a man's eyes before, not even in the eyes of a much younger and less experienced William. It suggested he had plans in mind that she didn't understand. The thought of whatever those plans entailed both frightened her and caused her heart to beat frantically.

Could he be married and still look at a woman that way? Probably so. Her mother had told her that men could be inconstant in their relationships with women.

She could *not* become involved with William again. She'd thought she'd never recover from the pain when he left her, from that innocent young love she'd believed they shared.

Oh, well, she thought briskly, she'd not worry about him any more tonight. She stood to allow Boswell to help her out of her dress and chemise and into a thick nightgown and robe. With warm slippers on her icy feet, Louisa sat in a large chair before the blazing fire, eating her dinner while her dresser continued to shake out her clothing and hang it up.

After an enormous yawn, Louisa said, "Boswell, you must be as tired as I am. Please get some dinner and go on to bed. I won't need you until morning."

With a bob, the dresser left and Louisa climbed into bed. But during the early hours, Louisa dreamed that a thin-faced man, eyes dark with emotion, kissed her. Louisa awakened, took a deep gasp of air, and crossed her arms over her chest. Would nothing rid her of his presence? He even invaded her dreams.

She realized she needed to take care of something. Throwing the covers back, she stood and padded across the dark room to where Boswell had placed her jewelry. She felt in a drawer for the key, then opened the box on top of the desk.

It contained little of value. She kept her most expensive jewelry in London and traveled with only gold bracelets, a garnet necklace and matching earrings, and a dainty gold ring in the shape of a rose that twined around her finger. She pulled the ring from the back of the box.

He had it made for her because they first met in a rose garden. The night before he left, he gave it to her. She'd worn it for two years, until she realized he would not come back. Then she'd tucked it in with her other jewelry and pretended it wasn't there. She rubbed her fingers over the flower but the rough edges scratched her, bringing a drop of blood.

What a fool she had been. What a fool she still was. Certainly eight years would be enough for most women to accept the fact that a man didn't care for her. Hadn't cared for her then, and hadn't thought about her since.

She walked to the fireplace, planning to toss the ring on the embers but couldn't. It was the last link between her and the lighthearted Louisa, between her staid existence and those days of unfettered joy, perhaps the only time she would ever experience love. Although she no longer inhabited that fantasy world, she couldn't destroy the only connection.

So she turned, walked back to the little box and dropped the ring inside before closing it, firmly, locking it with a determined twist and shutting the key in the drawer again.

Once back in bed, Louisa forced herself to fall asleep, replacing the dream of the young William with another one in which she carried a baby through the gardens of the estate.

Before the unexpected entrance of the woman he'd thought he'd vanquished from his thoughts long ago, William Rathe, Viscount Woodstone, had been in the parlor of his suite, watching the whirlpool made by swirling his brandy.

In the depths of the liquor, he had been contemplating the coil he'd landed in when he'd visited his friend

Arnold. Then the door to his bedroom opened. Startled, he'd looked though the open door between the parlor and the bedroom and saw a barefoot vision enter. She shook out splendid dark tresses which had led him to stand and move closer to admire the mysterious intruder. Then she threw her dark curls back. It had taken a few seconds before he was certain, but it was Louisa, muddied but still lovely.

The few times he'd thought of her in the last several years, he'd supposed her long married with a clutch of children. Perhaps she was. Perhaps she had escaped her husband and those clinging offspring. She was twenty-five. If she wasn't married, she'd be an old maid, but she didn't look like one.

The sight of him had shocked her, but Louisa had shown surprise only in a momentary intake of breath. She'd learned to disguise her feelings. A pity.

She'd changed in other ways. Of course she had. When he'd foolishly fallen in love with her, she'd been seventeen. Dewy and innocent but sweetly passionate. Now she was mature.

When they met, she'd been planning her season in London but was still somewhat coltish and gawky, just beginning to show the promise of the beautiful woman she'd become.

He'd been visiting a friend from Cambridge that summer. When they'd been invited to Louisa's father's estate for a Venetian breakfast, he'd wandered into the garden. There she stood, her back to him, that wonderful hair curling down her back in riotous profusion. He thought he'd never seen anything so lovely until she turned and gazed at him. She held a soft pink rose in her hand, the same color as her lips. Startled, she glanced up at him. For the first time, he saw her eyes, those beautiful blue-violet eyes that drew him toward her.

"Devil take it!" Why did he remember that after all this time? He didn't want to. The sight of her stirred memories and feelings better forgotten. He threw the glass of brandy against the fireplace and watched it shatter with satisfaction.

William came down to breakfast, a meal he'd become accustomed to eating alone since the departure of his hosts three days earlier. This morning, Louisa sat in *his* place, reading *his* newspaper. He could see a daintily curved wrist and delicate fingers holding the paper while a lacy cap showed above it. There was no ring on her finger, but she might for some reason not wear a wedding band.

"I did not realize you are Cassie's sister." He nodded at Louisa, who still hid behind the newspaper, before he picked up a plate and began to fill it from the dishes on the sideboard.

"How could you forget that?" She put down the newspaper. "Certainly you must have met her."

"You have a great many brothers and sisters, Louisa. I'm not even sure how many. Cassie must have been eleven or twelve when you and I knew each other. I don't even know if I met her, and she didn't remember me when I met her in London."

"But when she married Arnold, you must have—"

"You must remember I was not at the ceremony, and I don't study the bloodlines of my friends' brides."

"She was thirteen when we . . ." She sipped tea before she glanced up at him. "You had no idea I would be here?"

For a moment, he looked into her amazing eyes, now more blue than purple. He forced himself to look away. "Cassie said her sister was coming to help with the baby. I expected someone older. That was all I knew."

This morning, she was so completely and prudishly covered that he wondered if he'd imagined the sight of her, barefoot and disheveled. Gone was the gypsy. In her place was a woman who looked like a maiden aunt. But a maiden aunt of infinite possibilities, he thought, remembering the kisses they shared when they were young. He contemplated her thick, dark hair, curling where it escaped the engulfing lace of her cap. "Your husband does not travel with you?"

"I am not married." She didn't meet his eye as she spread marmalade on her muffin. "And your wife?"

"I do not have a wife."

Louisa glanced up at him. So, she thought, after all these years, he hadn't married. Odd, especially since he had acceded to the title. "I am sorry that your father and brother died. I did not know but assume they did, since you are the viscount."

"Yes. My father died of pneumonia two years ago. Tristan broke his neck hunting six months later."

"I am so sorry."

"Thank you." William took a bite of toast.

"Please accept my apology for invading your chambers last evening. I've always stayed there," Louisa said, and wished she could demand an apology for his ungentlemanly conduct of the previous evening. However, it would hardly be an elevating topic of conversation, and propriety had become an extremely important consideration for her in the past few years.

Instead, she folded the newspaper and placed it by her plate. "Will Lady Woolton join us for breakfast?"

"I have yet to see her. I believe she spends most of her time in her chambers."

Not much of a chaperone, Louisa considered, but enough for the rules of society. She searched for another topic of conversation. "Have you known Arnold for long?"

"We were at Cambridge together. In the past few years, we have seen each other only occasionally, so I was surprised when he wrote to request my presence here." He leaned forward to pick up the newspaper. "Arnold told me that Cassie's sister was somewhat straitlaced."

"Straitlaced?" She frowned, and paused with a bite of buttered eggs on her fork.

"Yes, you know: Prim, prudish, staid."

"Thank you." Louisa sniffed. *Oh, no,* she thought. *Certainly I didn't sniff, did I?* "I am well aware of what straitlaced means. I just haven't heard myself referred to as such, although it probably fits."

"You weren't so prim when we knew each other before, Louisa, and last night . . ."

"Before, I was a child; last night, you saw a tired woman."

"A vivid woman, full of life . . ."

"A woman who only wanted her bed and dinner." With that she pushed her chair back and stood with a quick and efficient movement. She picked up her cup and started to leave the room before she thought to ask for information. "I'm going to see the baby. Do you know whose child this is?"

"Her name is Beatrice."

"But why is she here? Who are her parents? Where are they? Why ever did they leave her with my flighty sister and her equally scatterbrained husband?"

"She was here when I arrived. I believe a friend of Arnold's is the father. I know little else. Your sister and Arnold asked me to stay until you took over. I am at your service and at little Beatrice's."

"Are you good with babies?" She took two steps toward him.

"As you know, I have a younger sister so, yes, I have some experience."

"Of course, you went away to school when you were six? Seven?" Louisa almost choked as he slowly studied a rebellious ringlet that had escaped from her cap and curled against her cheek. She longed to tuck it back but refused to allow him to disquiet her. Instead, she took a sip of her tea and allowed it to trickle down her throat. Did he still find her attractive? She shoved the traitorous thought back.

"When I was seven."

"Then you will not mind if I take over the care of the child?" She turned and strode toward the door, trying to get away from the effect the dratted man still had on her.

"Fine, I'll leave the child to you," he said to her back.

Louisa was entranced by Beatrice as soon as she saw her. Of course, this happened with every baby she held. "How old is she?" she asked Margaret, the pretty dark-haired nursery maid.

"Two months, my lady. At least, that's what we believe. When Beatrice arrived, we thought her mother would arrive soon, but she hasn't so we don't know her age exactly."

"She's such a sweet baby." Louisa took the infant in her arms, wrapped a blanket around the tiny form and cuddled her.

"Oh, yes, my lady. She sleeps and sleeps. But when she's awake, she loves to play and laugh." The nursery maid offered a thumb and the baby's tiny fingers wrapped around it.

"Lovey, lovey, lovey," Louisa, the doting maiden aunt, cooed to a quickly adopted niece. "She's beautiful. I believe I'll take her for a walk outside."

"Of course, my lady." Margaret hastened to put a ruffled bonnet on the baby's head.

"You seem to be very competent." Louisa studied the nursery maid. "I wonder why my sister felt it was necessary for the viscount and me to be here in her absence?"

Margaret glanced at Louisa quickly, her eyes wide and startled, then her gaze returned to the baby's face. "I'm sure I couldn't say, my lady."

As she strolled around the gardens with the baby, Louisa wondered if she had imagined the nursery maid's odd reaction to her question. Was Margaret hiding something?

That was absurd. What secrets would a nursery maid have? Then Bea gurgled and all thoughts except the delight of carrying the infant were forgotten.

Although Louisa spent much time over the next few days with Beatrice, she also visited Arnold's Aunt Felicia, a sweet but fuzzy-minded elderly lady who was content to stay in her suite.

During the next week, Louisa saw little of William. He spent the days riding around the estate and his evenings with friends in the area. Thus she ate alone or with Lady Woolton. Not that she missed his disturbing company, of course. It was comfortable not to be bothered by the blasted man whose self-assurance had grown three-fold in eight years, and who had changed so much from the younger son she'd loved that she wasn't even sure if she *liked* the man he'd become.

She also wondered why he stayed. However, because Lady Woolton acted as hostess during Arnold's absence, Louisa had no right to question his plans or reasons for remaining.

There was no repetition of the nursery maid's discomfort but there were odd times when Louisa carried little Bea around the estate and looked up to see William watching them from a balcony, or across a clearing, or from a post on the hillside opposite the gardens. She waved to him but he ignored her. Once when a carriage arrived with a visitor for tea, he thundered up behind it, pushing his mount so hard that the horse was covered with sweat. When he saw the guest was the squire's wife, he rode off without even greeting her. Very odd behavior.

And there was that singular incident. One afternoon Louisa paused before she entered the nursery and glanced through the open door. William stood with his arm around the shoulder of the nursery maid, his head bent toward her as Margaret leaned against him.

Louisa backed away as quickly and soundlessly as possible. She'd never thought William the type to trifle with a servant, certainly not when visiting a friend's estate, but she didn't know him anymore. Was Bea his daughter?

Oh, certainly not. She couldn't believe that he'd

leave his illegitimate child with Cassie, but why was William holding Margaret?

Why was he still here?

And who was the baby?

Chapter Three

One beautiful sunny afternoon a week after her arrival at Longtrees, several of the ladies of the neighborhood arrived for tea and a comfortable coze. After that, they enjoyed a pleasant stroll in the rose garden, wandering through the beautifully kept flower beds, delighting in the view of the lake, and resting in the summerhouse to continue their discussion of the latest news and gossip from London.

"Why, look up there, Louisa," said Lady Mary Wortham, a friend from early days. "I believe there is someone over there, watching us."

Louisa looked where her friend pointed. She could see the glitter of light hitting glass—a spyglass? Was it William?

Several of the other guests laughed and pointed.

"Perhaps a disappointed suitor, Louisa?" teased one.

At last they agreed it was probably a hunter or a lover of nature. As they conversed, Louisa found herself glancing at the hillside, wondering about the person there until, after fifteen minutes, the reflections on the hill disappeared.

William watched the women from the distance. Obviously friends visiting Louisa, but he wished them elsewhere, away from the danger he knew lay in wait around Longtrees.

And here he was, alone to attempt to protect the treasure that slept in the nursery. Well, not completely alone. With the departure of Cassie and Arnold, he had Louisa to help him.

Blast Arnold for saddling him with Louisa! He wouldn't have minded if she was the woman he'd known years ago. That woman had fire and courage and could handle the ordeal he feared lay ahead, but Louisa had become, well, there was the only word for it— prim! If there was danger, and he feared there would be, how would she react? Probably faint at the first brush with trouble and need to be revived. He cursed the circumstances that had pitched him into the middle of a crisis and with only Miss Prim as his partner. "Bah!"

Remembering he was not completely dependent upon Louisa's strong right arm, that there was one man in the area he could count on, William spun, leaped on Charger, and rode from the clearing to meet his confederate.

Considering the fact that she was preparing for only a country assembly, Louisa dressed with care the next evening. She told herself William was definitely not the reason she put on her most fashionable rose satin underdress covered with a flattering lacy overdress. No, he certainly was not, she reminded herself as she admired Boswell's handiwork in the mirror.

Her hair looked lovely—almost a shame to cover it with a cap except that this one was quite flattering. Deciding not to ruin the lovely curls her dresser had arranged, she tossed the cap on the bed and descended to join William.

"I do hope you have saved me a dance," William said politely as he escorted her from the carriage into the assembly rooms.

"As you requested," she stated before the other young men of the district besieged her.

Louisa had often said that rural assembly rooms reminded her a great deal of Almack's, the place to be seen in London: the decor was not particularly elegant and the refreshments were not tempting. However, she enjoyed Arnold's neighbors greatly, which far outweighed the ordinary surroundings and uninspired refreshments—not, of course, that she would mention that to Arnold's neighbors.

When William appeared at her side for his dance, she

realized she'd been tinglingly aware of his presence even before he spoke, and chided herself. Tall and thin in his unadorned black formal attire, he was not handsome, but certainly extremely attractive.

Their dance started a terrible fluttering inside her. As they began the steps of a country dance, she remembered the words of her sister Cassie when she first met Arnold. "He makes my heart go pitty-pat," she'd said.

"Pitty-pat," Louisa had sniffed then but, when William took her hand and led her to the floor, she knew exactly what Cassie had meant, and was reminded of a much younger Louisa whose heart had also gone pitty-pat when she'd danced with William. How could a touch on the hand, and a soft breath against her cheek cause such tumult?

But her heart was much more mature now. She was no longer that young Louisa. She ordered her heart to behave itself and those foolish pitty-pats stopped immediately.

The steps of the dance made conversation impossible although they chatted about acquaintances while they awaited their turn to dance through the aisle created by the other dancers.

"Are you enjoying yourself?" she asked.

"Do you mean here, at the assembly? Or at Longtrees?"

"Either. I would not think a country assembly would be to your liking."

"Have I shown myself so hard to please? A country

assembly is a wonderful place to see who is in the vicinity. It is much to my liking."

"And Longtrees? Are you enjoying yourself there? I do not see how you could. We never see you."

"Do you miss me?"

He turned his obsidian eyes on her, the eyes that had caused a younger Louisa to sigh but did not affect her well-armored heart at all.

"Certainly not, but you have been a most unusual guest."

"Perhaps you would have preferred me to stay at Longtrees and dance attendance on you?" He quickly became serious. "I've been doing everything I can for little Bea. I hope I need never tell you what that is."

When he didn't explain that cryptic remark, Louisa again attended to the steps of the dance.

As the music ended and William took her to her seat, he asked, "Has your sister written? Do you know when they return?"

"No. Cassie writes only in extreme emergencies so I do not expect to hear from her."

He nodded and turned from her.

"Please tell me," she began before he could move away. "Why do you watch us?"

"My lady, I've only been keeping an eye on other points of interest in the neighborhood."

Before she could ask what he meant, her next partner claimed Louisa, but she noticed William danced only a few more times. The rest of the evening he spent talking with men, those in the card room and those standing around the edges of the floor. It was odd, as if he was seeking information instead of disporting himself at a rural assembly.

Louisa was to remember William's odd words two evenings later and wondered if they had been a warning.

After dinner, it was her habit to stroll through the gardens on Arnold's estate. When Cassie was in residence, the two sisters liked to gossip while they walked along the twisting paths, or to sit in the summerhouse and chatter.

This evening, Louisa wandered through the rose garden, then seated herself on a bench overlooking the lake, enjoying the scented air that floated on a cool breeze. As she sat there, time passed and the evening grew darker. She knew she should return but there was nothing of interest for her in the house, no one to keep her company. Hours spent in the drawing room would be filled with reading or embroidery. Neither interested her as much as the garden.

Then she heard the sound of someone walking in the lower garden. Oh, not someone moving quickly and breaking branches, but soft footsteps and rustling, as if someone attempted to move quietly through the brush and across the paths.

"William, is that you?" she called.

No one answered, but the sounds stopped.

If it was William, why hadn't he answered? And, if it wasn't, who was it?

Well, it was probably an animal, maybe a fox searching for a tasty meal.

A little frightened by her imagination but certain she could not be in danger—not on Arnold's estate—Louisa continued to inhale the scented air and delight in the fragrant evening. However, just in case, she also listened intently and, after a few minutes, stood to walk toward the mansion.

Only moments later, the sounds started again.

"Who is that?" she shouted, dreadfully frightened at the thought of being alone in the garden while someone prowled through the brush. Then she scolded herself for allowing whoever skulked to know she was still there. She should have stayed quiet so the person would pass on.

With her narrow skirt and flimsy shoes, she knew she could not outrun whoever lurked out there. Perhaps if she moved slowly and quietly, she could get to the house before the intruder found her.

Could this have anything to do with Bea? Oh, how could it? Her imagination was running away with her again.

When the sound came closer, she started to run. Then someone grabbed her arm and dragged her against him with callused hands. The scent of his dirty, sweaty body made her sick and the roughness of his clothing scratched her. She screamed and, with all her might, Louisa fought but he slapped her hard. She couldn't get her hands free and her legs were tangled in her dress, but she bent her knees then stood quickly to butt his chin with her head.

"Stop!" she shouted. "Help!" But the back of the house was dark. No one could hear her screams.

The man tried to cover her mouth but she bit his hand. Taking advantage of his momentary distraction, Louisa wrested her right arm free, turned and clawed his face, then put her thumb in his eye and pushed as hard as she could, a tactic she'd learned from her eldest nephew. The man let go.

Kicking off her shoes, Louisa ran up the path. She knew she'd not make it to the house. She could hear his jagged breathing closing in behind her.

Her knowledge of the grounds was to her advantage, her only advantage she thought as she heard his feet pounding behind her. Louisa sidestepped a row of rose bushes and heard the man blunder into them seconds later. She ran on, increasing the distance between them. As she rounded the side of the house, she could see only light that filtered through the parlor windows. She screamed again but no one looked out at her.

She hadn't realized how large the house was until now, until she raced around it with the harsh breathing of her pursuer sounding closer and closer. She could see the drive ahead but knew she'd not arrive there before he caught up with her. She wasn't sure she could run that far because the rough paths of the garden had cut her feet and her sides hurt so much she could barely draw a breath.

When she looked back, trying to glimpse him in the dark, she tripped over something—a branch she discovered as she felt for it. She stood and picked the branch up in one movement then dashed behind a statue where she stopped, forcing herself to calm her heavy breathing so he'd not know she lay in wait for him. When she heard his footsteps approach, Louisa lifted the branch and swung it neck high. It hit the man with a satisfying thwack. Not waiting to investigate, she turned and ran again, dashing around the corner of the house and toward the front door where she saw William standing on the steps, a cigar in his hand.

Thank goodness! Louisa stopped. She was safe. "William!" she shouted before she began to shake and cry.

"What happened Louisa?"

She took a deep breath and tried to stop crying. "There was a man out there." She pointed. "He tried to grab me."

"Where?" His voice was rough and angry.

"In the garden. He followed me to the side of the house but I hit him with a branch."

"Did he hurt you?" He held her shoulders and looked into her face, studying a cut on her cheek.

"A little, but I'm fine." Her cheek throbbed and her feet hurt so much she wasn't sure she could walk anymore, but she really was fine knowing she was safe, and that William would protect her.

William dropped her arm, his face suffused with anger. "I will leave you to get into the house yourself while I see who this man is and why he has attacked you." He ran into the darkened garden.

She hobbled up to the top step where she sat and cried. While she awaited William's return, Louisa attempted to gain control of her emotions. She could hear scuffling sounds, first close to the house then moving away. Then there was silence. When he appeared on the drive almost fifteen minutes later, there was a small cut across his chin. "Did you find him?"

"Yes, he was only a ruffian, looking for money. I am sorry you were so frightened. Are you hurt?"

"Mostly frightened."

For a moment, she thought his eyes flashed in anger, but it was dark and she couldn't tell. Maybe it was the way his body had tensed when she'd confessed her fear, but somehow she knew he was furious.

"I'm sorry that happened. After I hit him a few times, he got away." William shook his head. "I wish I could have taken him to the bailiff."

"Will he return?"

"No," he said forcefully.

"Does this have anything to do with the baby?" She could feel his stare but he didn't answer for almost a minute.

"Why would you think that, Louisa?"

"There are so many mysteries, William. Who is the baby? Why is she here? Who is this man who grabbed me?"

"Louisa, that is foolishness. Bea is only a baby, visiting until her parents return. The man who attacked you was a vagrant, probably a former soldier, looking for food or money."

He was lying, she knew that but she also knew he wouldn't answer her. She glared at him in the darkness then turned to enter the house and limp upstairs.

Chapter Four

Louisa was in the nursery with Bea the morning after the incident with the ruffian, as William had called him, but Louisa did not believe the designation. Suddenly, Margaret, the nursery maid, dashed in, sobbing with her hands clutched in front of her. "They're almost here, Lady Louisa. The viscount says you must take little Bea and leave immediately."

Feeling as if she'd stumbled into one of Cassie's gothic novels, Louisa stared at the frightened maid. "What do you mean? Who's coming? What's all this about William and me and the baby?"

"He didn't tell you, did he?" Margaret shook her head. "I was afraid he wouldn't, but her ladyship said I should trust him to. Lady Louisa, you must take Bea and leave now! They're coming!"

Totally confused by what the maid said and certain the poor woman must be crazy, Louisa placed the baby in the crib and slowly approached Margaret to calm her.

At that moment, William entered the nursery and demanded, "Where's the baby? Is she ready to go?"

"I'll get her milk and some clothes, but Lady Louisa—"

"I'll take care of Lady Louisa while you get the baby ready." He watched Margaret begin the preparations before turning toward Louisa.

Louisa opened her mouth to tell him what she thought of his I'll-take-care-of-Lady-Louisa statement but the stern look in his dark eyes checked her words.

"I haven't time to explain because I'd hoped this wouldn't happen. I believed they wouldn't find her but I fear they have. You and I have to take Bea away from here now, before they surround the estate." He spoke rapidly and with such great authority that Louisa was nearly convinced she had to do whatever he expected.

"Who wants Bea? And why?" Louisa asked. "Where are we going?"

"I don't have time to explain." He strode to the door then paused to wait for Louisa.

"The baby's too young to travel," Louisa protested.

"She's not too young to die. We must leave. Now."

"What do you mean she's not too young to die?"

"Louisa, there isn't time. Trust me. We have to leave and now!" He took her arm and hustled her down the hall toward her room. "Change into your riding habit and meet me at the stable within five minutes. Can you do that?"

"Well, of course I can." Louisa nodded and dashed into her room, propelled by his repeated use of the word 'now,' spoken in a voice that brooked no disagreement. She told Boswell to pack a clean petticoat and chemise in a hatbox while she undressed. That completed, Boswell helped her into her riding habit.

"I don't understand what you're doing, Lady Louisa," said Boswell as she buttoned the front of the habit. "Taking off like this. I should be going along. How will I explain your departure to your sister?"

Louisa pulled on her boots. "From the way the viscount talked, Cassie and Arnold know what's going on and will understand." She stood. "I'm sure we shan't be gone long. It's not what I would like, but this seems to be an emergency." Louisa jammed on the jaunty hat that matched the trim on the handsome dark green habit. "We have to take the baby to another place, probably to another estate. I'll insist we spend the night there, well-chaperoned. I do hate to think of paying a visit with only my riding habit." Louisa looked down at the fashionable garment with its gold braid and buttons.

Boswell sniffed.

"Don't worry. I'm sure we'll be back tomorrow." She pulled on her gloves, took the hatbox from Boswell and hurried down the stairs. She walked as quickly as the rules of etiquette allowed to the stable, still moved by the urgency in William's voice. The two arrived at the stable at the same time.

He took Charger from the stable boy, who also led a frisky mare.

"Her name is Bess, my lady," the stable boy said.

"Can you ride astride?" William demanded of Louisa.

"I can ride anything with four legs."

"I sent an order down for two horses but didn't specify one should have a lady's saddle. We don't have time to change."

With another don't-argue-Louisa glare, William made a foothold and threw Louisa onto the horse. She settled herself across the mare but found even the full skirt of her habit didn't stretch enough for her to put both feet in the stirrups.

Seeing her dilemma, William said, "Lean forward." He grabbed the back of her skirt and petticoat and ripped until the material was loose enough for her to be properly mounted.

Louisa had begun to protest but, before the words were out, the ruin of her clothing was complete. How would she explain that to her hosts this evening?

However, his action solved the problem. She tugged until the extra material covered her and fell to the top of her boots. She tried to get used to the animal's body between her legs while balancing the hatbox. Then William tied a bundle on his horse and leaped on him, just as Margaret appeared with Bea and a bag which she handed to William.

But Charger began to sidle, bothered by the fluttering bag which the horse could see out of the side of his eye. "Take this." William stretched out a hand that held Bea's essentials.

"And where should I put it?" she asked sweetly.

"Give me the hatbox and take this!"

Acquiescing to the force of his words, she handed him the hatbox and took the baby's possessions. To her dismay, he took her clothing out of the hatbox and stuffed it in his bundle. Then he retied the bundle to Charger and tossed the box to the ground before he took the baby from Margaret.

"Be careful with her, my lord," the nursery maid said.

Then Louisa and William rode off at top speed.

It was amazing how quickly one obeyed a voice like William's. Of course, no one had ever shouted at her before so that was a new experience, not one she desired to repeat.

Suddenly, now that her mind had stopped reeling from the escape, she realized that she was alone with William, with only a baby as company, exactly the situation Boswell had been so concerned about. "How long are we going to ride?" she shouted at William who didn't hear her, her words drowned out by the wind and the hoofbeats.

He rode ahead of her, his broad shoulders jutting out, dark hair curling a little over the collar of his jacket, exuding a masculinity that even at this distance was almost overwhelming. This man who was once *her* William still attracted her tremendously. He must never know she was still such a fool.

Surely they must be close to their destination, her thoughts continued. They couldn't be out here alone in this wilderness for much longer without destroying her reputation.

But, of course, this wasn't a wilderness. This was England. People were all around. She might not be able to see them but she knew there were farms behind the hedgerow. And she had faith that the people in the unseen cottages would protect her were this man to try to ravish her.

In addition, she couldn't forget that the man who rode ahead of her was a friend of Arnold's and had once been dear to her. Despite his breaking her heart, she had always thought him a man of honor. She knew he would do nothing to harm her. Besides, there was really no choice now.

They didn't rest for hours. A few times, William stopped and turned, not to check on Louisa but as if to listen. Most of the time they rode as hard as the horses would take them until the baby awoke and began to sob noisily. No matter how much William jiggled and tried to soothe her, she only cried harder.

"She won't stop until she's cared for, you know,"

Louisa said as she pulled her mount next to William's. "She's hungry and probably uncomfortably wet."

"I know she's wet," he said with a grimace as he slowed his mount and turned off the road. "She's thoroughly soaked my arm, but we couldn't slow down before now."

He dismounted with the baby in his arm. "Do you need help?" he asked as she remained on Bess' back.

The unaccustomed riding position had caused her legs to ache but, preferring excruciating pain to admitting a weakness to this demanding and very military William, she twisted, lifted her leg over the saddle and slowly let herself down. Although she stumbled when her legs touched ground, she held onto the saddle, righted herself, and explained, "I'm not used to dismounting like this. Now, let me change her." Her voice was steady and full of her usual authority.

She took Bea and the packet. Biting her lip against the aching of her legs, she searched for and found a clean, grassy place where she removed the baby's clothing, thankful for the sunshine of this warm autumn day.

"She's wet all through. I hope Margaret packed another dress." Finding what she needed in the bundle, she said, "I'll put two cloths on her this time. While I'm doing this, I would appreciate if you'd explain to me why we have dashed off in this higgety-piggety manner? You act as if the devil himself were after us."

"He may well be," William said as he strode to the

road and looked back. "Margaret is not a nursery maid. She's the wife of our most valued English spy who now is deep in France."

Louisa gasped.

"He's safe where he is, sending back important information. Someone told the French the location of our spy's baby daughter."

"Beatrice?"

"Yes. This makes him very vulnerable on this end. If his daughter is kidnapped, Boney has a trump card."

"Oh my." Louisa sat back on her heels to listen.

"That's why Arnold and I moved them to Longtrees where we thought they'd be safe. Last night, you surprised one of the spies."

"So that man wasn't a ruffian?"

"No, he was looking for Beatrice. He might have gotten in the house if you hadn't alerted me. Unfortunately, he got away before I could question him. This morning, the man I set to watch the roads saw a group of riders approaching the estate."

"Wouldn't it have been better to hold them off on the estate?"

"How would we do that?" William gave her a withering glance. "Longtrees is not a fortress. The men living there have no experience in fighting men like these."

"But with you and your men—"

"I have no army, just one man. There are few I can trust with knowledge about Beatrice so we're limited in manpower. My man and I would not be able to keep a group of traitors away without many injuries, perhaps the loss of our lives, and the life of the baby. Our only hope is to outride them."

"Isn't Margaret in danger also? Why didn't we bring her?"

"Margaret is safe because the servants believe she is the baby's nurse. In addition, the birth was too difficult to allow her to ride as hard as we must. That is why you're here."

"I did wonder the reason for that." Finished changing the baby, she soaked a clean napkin in milk and allowed Beatrice to suck on it contentedly.

"As you pointed out, I have little experience with children whereas you have a great deal. We'd planned on your sister caring for her, but when Arnold had to leave, we needed to find another woman to care for the child." He nodded at Bea. "Cassie said you are wonderful with children and would love an adventure."

"I must thank Cassie for that," Louisa said acerbically, then asked, "And yet you told me nothing of this?"

"I had hoped it wouldn't be necessary. I've always thought that the fewer people who knew, the easier it was to keep a secret. Nor was I sure—" He looked over his shoulder at her.

"Nor were you sure I'd welcome this escapade? Nor how I would behave?" she finished for him. "Perhaps you thought I'd swoon or fall off the horse? You must have wondered how this maiden aunt could possibly become a fearless adventuress who would not hinder you." She considered for a moment. "I'm not sure I blame you. Nonetheless, I would have *liked* to be consulted."

As the baby finished sucking the milk and settled into a happy sleep, Louisa tried to stand. However, her aching legs didn't allow this with the baby in her arms so she asked, "Would you take her while I gather everything together?" Holding onto a low branch, she stood, then noticed a creek at the edge of the clearing. "I'll rinse this wet cloth out for later. Would you like me to wash the sleeve of your jacket?"

He looked down at what was once a handsome coat but was now wrinkled and emitted a terrible stench. "I don't think it would help," he said as he took the sleeping infant. "We probably should get on the road as soon as you're ready."

While she washed the cloth, Louisa looked up at William. "We've been riding a long time. When will we get where we're going? Will it take much longer?"

"I don't know."

"Where are we going?"

"I don't know."

"What?" Louisa sat up so quickly she almost lost the cloth down the stream. She reached for it and wrung it out before she turned to confront William. "What do you mean you don't know where we are going?"

"I don't know where to take Bea." William turned away from Louisa. "Every place I know is unsafe: My friends and family are well known to these spies. Your sister had an idea, an old nurse of hers, but I don't know where she lives."

"She lives in Bury-Saint-Edmund. We have gone the opposite direction. Why didn't you ask me how to get there sooner?" Pushing herself up by the adjacent tree, she stood.

"There wasn't time. We rode hard and fast to get away from the estate as quickly as possible. Direction didn't matter."

"Well, it does now. This was not well planned. Hadn't you and Arnold and Cassie thought this through at all?"

"Yes, we'd planned to take her to another estate where we thought she'd be safe, but yesterday I received a message that there were strangers there as well."

"I wish you had mentioned this before we left. We won't get to Mopsie's home today, even if we turned around immediately."

"Which we cannot do, else we'll run into the men we're trying to escape." He rubbed his horse's shoulder. "No, the plan wasn't well conceived, but there wasn't much time."

"Would you please face me while we're talking?"

When William turned toward her, Louisa continued. "The problem arose because you didn't trust your collaborator."

"That's not entirely true."

"Oh, I think so. Had high-spirited Cassie and daring

Arnold been here, you would have discussed everything beforehand, but you didn't want to work with me. You allowed your prejudice to overcome your judgment and placed an innocent babe in a precarious position. Also, and of less importance, you have harmed irrevocably the reputation of the person who should have been your confidant in this harebrained scheme. I could not have blundered anymore than you have."

"Louisa, we need not lay blame at this time. Rest assured, I will do the proper thing to restore your reputation."

"And what is that?" she asked with deceptive calm.

"I'll marry you, devil take it. What did you think?"

"Oh, you'll marry me—devil take it?" She didn't bother to disguise the venom in her voice. "Thank you. I should be delighted to receive such a heartfelt declaration. It is every girl's dream, devil take it! But you need not fear. I have no more desire to marry you than you have to marry me."

She finishing wringing the cloth out while she reordered her thoughts. "Since we cannot arrive at Mopsie's today, I'd like to go to an estate, any estate, this afternoon. There I may pretend my reputation is not completely destroyed."

"Impossible. Bea is still in danger. I know nothing about any estates around here. We could easily walk into a trap. It's time to go. Now."

She wished she could fling the wet cloth in his face and jump on her horse, leaving William alone in this venture, but two thoughts kept her from doing this. First, she couldn't leave Bea when danger threatened. The second was more personal and humiliating. She didn't know if she could mount the horse on her own.

After William tossed Louisa onto Bess and mounted his horse holding the baby, they rode slowly and silently. The wet cloth lay across the neck of her mount while his jacket draped across the rump of his steed.

Riding for hours behind William and Bea, Louisa became more and more aware of her aching legs. Although the pace had slowed to rest the animals, the unaccustomed rubbing of the saddle on the soft flesh of her thighs was chafing them unbearably. She would not complain! No, never to that straight-backed man who hadn't wanted her to come in the first place. She'd bear it until they had Bea out of harm's way. The infant's welfare had to be her first priority. Surreptitiously she wiggled and tugged until the thin muslin of the petticoat separated the two surfaces and cut down on the agonizing rubbing.

Louisa realized that it was necessary to restore at least a semblance of communication with William. Possibly, if she talked to him, he might allow her input into his plans, non-existent as they were. In addition, it was the proper thing for a lady to do. What could she talk to the arrogant fellow about? She saw William's coat and called out genially, "You'll not be able to wear that coat again without smelling like wet horse."

"And wet baby," he agreed. "No, they won't let me into Almack's in this. Not that I'd go were they to ask me."

Louisa decided that it would be easy to talk to William if she pretended he was her brother-in-law Arnold or her eldest nephew just down from Oxford, instead of her former love and her present abductor. "Ah, you're not involved in London society?"

"No, but mostly I'm not much interested in the marriage mart."

Concluding marriage was a more personal topic, and one she didn't want to explore, Louisa asked, "Why haven't I seen you in London? Our world is fairly small. Certainly our paths should have crossed again before this."

William slowed his horse to ride next to her.

"Well, after I left your estate, my father bought me my colors. He thought serving on the peninsula would be a good education for me. When I returned, he sent me to the former colonies to work with my uncle in Boston, still hoping to make of me the man he wanted me to be."

"Did it?" Louisa subtly changed positions.

"I think he really meant that time in Boston as punishment. I liked it and learned a great deal but spent several years away from London. Last season I spent in Scotland with friends. However, sometime between those, I was in London."

"And during at least two of those, I had a sister or sister-in-law increasing and only passed the little season in London. Oh, and there was the time all of my nieces and nephews had spots, and I traveled among the estates. Well, that explains why we didn't meet each other again, until now."

They spent the next few hours in sporadic conversation until they rested a few minutes to feed and change Bea and to rinse out her cloths. It was late afternoon when they stopped for the day.

"It's a little earlier than I wanted to stop." He turned his horse into an abandoned farm. "But I hate to ride further with the baby, and this is what I've been looking for, a place where no one will see us." He dismounted, tied Charger to a tree then placed Bea in a pile of hay inside a tumbledown shed. "May I help you dismount? You must be stiff after riding all day."

"Of course not. I'm fine. Certainly not happy to be spending the night here. But"—she sniffed—"I will survive."

Barely able to lift her right leg, Louisa twisted in the saddle and tried to let herself down slowly but, when her feet hit the ground, she couldn't stop herself. She slid slowly to the ground where she lay biting her lip.

"Louisa, what have you done to yourself?" He rushed over to help her stand, but she refused to let him touch her.

"I am just a *little* sore. Go away." She waved her hand at him. "I can take care of myself." She grabbed the stirrup, pulled herself up, took a step and steadied herself against Bess, then turned to hobble toward the small shed.

William cursed to himself when he saw blood on the thin petticoat as she limped away from him. How badly was she hurt? Could they go on? "Louisa?"

Louisa looked back at the sound of his voice and noticed the direction of his gaze, then attempted to close the split skirt. Not even recognizing the impropriety of his concern, he pushed the skirt of the riding habit aside to study her legs.

"What have you done to yourself?" he demanded.

"Sir!" Louisa protested. She pushed him away and slapped his hand. "Do not touch me!"

"Be quiet! I'm not going to ravish you, for God's sake!" William picked Louisa up and lay her down gently on the hay next to Bea. Louisa attempted to move away, pushing herself a short distance with her feet but he grabbed her skirt and hauled her back to where he knelt.

"Now, be still and let me look at this." With the heavy merino out of the way, he tried to lift the thin material of the petticoat from her legs but it was embedded in the large sores which covered her inner thighs. With a whistle, he shook his head. "Why didn't you tell me?"

"We had to get Bea away. You said—"

"But this! How could you ride?" When she didn't answer, he took out his knife and cut away what material he could, not attempting to remove the sections that would be too painful to tear away. He looked up at her, amazed, but she couldn't meet his eyes and her cheeks were pink.

He'd thought she'd become a proper old maid, but he had to admire her courage. Louisa was still pluck to the core.

"You know, I saw heroism on the peninsula but that a person could ride while in such pain, well, I'm astonished. I'm sorry I doubted." He studied the sores. "I was wrong and beg you will forgive me for my prejudice and for causing you such discomfort and dishonor." He then spoke with such gentleness that she turned to look at him. "I'm going to have to get this cloth out of these wounds or they'll putrefy but I need water or salve to soften them." He stood. "I'll have to find a farm and see what I can borrow."

She sat up. "No! They'll remember us! You can't chance that!"

"I have to get milk for Bea and food for us. I'll ask for salve while I'm there. I'll walk or else someone might see and remember Charger. I might be gone for some time." He stretched and looked around them. "Neither the house nor the barn have roofs, so I fear we'll have to stay in this outbuilding. First, I'll settle the horses, then I'll be back."

"Let me move you into the shed," he said when he returned a few minutes later with his bundle and Bea's. He settled Bea in her arms in the filthy but seemingly solid structure and brought more straw for their comfort. "Do you think you'll be able to take care of her while I'm gone?"

"Of course."

"Let me leave you one of my pistols."

"No, thank you." She turned back to the baby.

"You might need it."

"I doubt if it would be useful. I don't know how to use one and would probably severely injure one of us."

By the time William returned, Louisa had decided she really couldn't care for the baby by herself. The last of the milk smelled bad and, although normally the most placid of infants, when hungry Beatrice was a terror. Louisa changed and sang to the child but Bea screamed so loudly Louisa feared their pursuers would hear her from miles away.

Even an effort to walk Bea hadn't helped because Louisa discovered to her chagrin that she could not stand by herself. Not only did the wounds hurt, but the muscles of her legs had tightened unmercifully.

"I didn't have to go far." William finally strode into the building and placed a basket on the ground next to Louisa. "I found milk for the baby, some cheese and bread for us, and two blankets, but all I could get was water for your legs."

"I'm sure that will be fine," Louisa stated, delighted to see the small container of milk.

After Louisa fed Bea, the baby fell into a contented slumber. The adults ate, then William turned again to Louisa's sores. Because he obviously saw her not as a woman but a comrade in arms, and because she knew her legs had to be cared for and she couldn't possibly do it herself, she tried to shed her modesty. In spite of her resolve, it was impossible to remain passive to the clinical yet intimate touch of this man.

Louisa shut her eyes, took a deep breath, and pretended this man whom she had once loved was not really touching her where no one—*no one*—had touched her as long as she could remember.

With tender care, he soaked the petticoat that clung to the bleeding gashes on her legs with water, and pulled the fabric away slowly and gently. In spite of his great care, Louisa had to bite her lip to keep from crying out.

"I think that's got it," he said, then reached in his pack for a bottle. "Brandy. It should help."

"Shouldn't I have drunk it before you started?"

"No," he said with a smile. "I am not talking about your being intoxicated. I'll use it on the sores. On the peninsula, wounds washed in spirits always seemed to do better."

She again bit her lip to keep from whimpering at the sting of the alcohol.

"Did you bring another petticoat?"

"Yes, you placed it in your bundle."

"Good." He turned toward their possessions, opened the packet, and felt for the soft material of her clothing. He pulled out the petticoat and shoved the other things back in his bundle. Then he glanced back at Louisa, resting in the straw with her eyes closed. He wished she was back in the parlor at Longtrees.

"William? Can't you find them?"

"I had another idea. We can't let those legs rub together." He held up his unmentionables. "These should help."

"No, that is not at all necessary," she stated as he began to tear her petticoat into strips.

"Of course it is," he insisted as he wound the material around her legs. "Tomorrow I want you to wear these." He motioned to his trousers. "That should give you some padding, so the pain won't be as bad as it could be."

"They are much too big, William. I'll feel foolish."

He studied them for a minute, then pulled the knife from the packet on Charger. "I'll slit them here." He made some holes around the waist with the knife. "Then put some rope through them. I saw some in the barn. You can tie them around your waist. As for feeling foolish, who will see you?"

"That is true. Now, would you help me stand?"

"Certainly not! Why do you need to get up?"

"Because, as helpful as you have been, there are certain needs I must take care of for myself."

"Louisa, you must let me help you. You can't walk far."

"I appreciate your kindness. This is something I must do for myself and by myself."

"Didn't you leave off, 'young man?' "

"What do you mean?"

"Didn't you mean to say, 'I appreciate your kindness, young man, but this is something I must do myself?' "

She laughed, a delightful sound that sparkled in the darkness of the abandoned shed. "I do sound like an old maid at times, don't I? As if I were speaking to my nephews. I apologize, but, please, if you will help me up and walk me to a private place, then leave me, that I would appreciate."

Louisa fed Bea once more that night before she settled the baby in the straw next to her.

William's voice came from the shadows. "I suggest you not take off your boots or clothing. We may have to leave quickly."

In the dark, she could hear him settling himself. In the thick darkness that enfolded them, she became even more aware there were only the two of them and a baby. And she was frightened again.

She sat, straight and unwavering as she'd been taught a lady sits, her legs held as tightly together as the pain allowed. Surely she could trust him. He'd always been a gentleman with her. However, some men, her mother had told her, were unpredictable creatures. She hadn't seen him in years. Perhaps *he* had become an unpredictable creature.

"Miss Prim?"

"Are you addressing me, William?"

"I believe there is no one else here unless Beatrice began to talk while I was away."

"Yes, William?"

"Louisa, you can relax now and go to sleep. You know me well enough to realize you have nothing to fear from me. I promise I will refrain from ravishing you."

"Thank you for your assurance. I, of course, had no doubt of your trustworthiness." She lay down, pulled Bea into the curve of her arm and relaxed her screaming muscles as much as possible, but she remained awake until William's gentle snores told her he was asleep.

Chapter Five

Louisa awoke, a piece of straw tickling her nose. She lay in the peaceful darkness for a few moments until she heard a rustling sound from outside. Quickly awake, she sat up slowly and touched the baby next to her. Satisfied that Bea was there and sleeping, she stood, ignoring the pain and stiffness in her legs, and looked to the dark corner. She could make out a lump where William lay. Unfortunately, he was too far away to awaken without making a great deal of noise.

With her left hand, she steadied herself on the rickety wall of the shelter. With the right, she searched for a weapon against the intruder outside. All she found was a splintery old board. When she tested it against the floor, the plank seemed solid. Moving slowly and quietly toward the door, she saw a figure silhouetted against the first light of dawn. She leaned against the flimsy wall of the shack, ready to protect the child.

As she tiptoed through the refuse on the floor, her foot collided with something hard. Ignoring the jagged pain which traveled from her toe up her aching legs, she stooped and picked up whatever it was she'd kicked and tossed it in William's direction to alert him, but it fell far short.

"Wake up, Louisa," a voice called from outside. The silhouette became William, who strode into the shed, saw the plank in her hands and smiled. "Do you always go after men with a board? Perhaps that explains your unmarried state."

Louisa ignored the statement. "I didn't know who it was." She glanced over to where he had slept and realized the lump she'd assumed was William was a pile of straw.

"Ahh. I feel safer knowing that you are ready to do battle against the foe with whatever weapon is at hand."

Louisa threw the board down and shouted, "I am *not* used to this, you know! I've never played the war games you men take so seriously. The baby and I have been caught up in this idiocy, and I am doing my very best."

She was immediately appalled at her words. How rude to shriek like a harridan. How unladylike, and yet it felt incredibly emancipating.

"Yes, you are. I apologize for jesting. Neither am I used to being caught up in such a game; at least, not

with a woman and a baby along. I appreciate your vigilance and will try to remember to communicate with
you better."

"I believe we'd both appreciate that." She glanced at
the sleeping baby. What an amazingly good child. How
could she have slumbered through the racket? "Shall
we get started while Bea's still asleep? Will you please
saddle my horse for me while I dress and gather her
things?" Louisa gasped when she looked at the state of
her riding habit and began to pick and brush the dried
grass from the thick fabric.

On the straw were the unmentionables William had
left for her to cover the wounds on her thighs. Men's
clothing headed a list of things she did not want to
wear, but her legs already hurt. Certainly, comfort was
more important than propriety and the desire to appear
ladylike.

She pulled the garment on and tied it in place, thankful that the high waist of her habit allowed the addi-
tional bulk. After a tentative step, she sighed. The
unmentionables did help. She could ride without the
terrible pain.

"I've found a vehicle," William called.

"A vehicle?" She picked pieces of straw from the
skirt in an effort to improve her appearance.

"There was a wagon in one of the farm buildings and
some old traces, and I bought a horse. Both Bess and
Charger will follow along. You'll ride in comfort
today." He tied their riding horses on the back of the

wagon then hitched the large black horse to the wagon and tossed some straw, the saddles, and their few possessions in the back.

"But it will slow us down! I can ride, I promise I'll be fine." Deciding she had cleaned her disreputable dress as much as possible, she attempted the impossible chore of patting and poking her hair in place.

"That's not necessary, Louisa. No one passed during the night so I believe we've lost them, at least for now. Although we still must get Beatrice to safety, I believe we do not have to travel so fast. You must agree the wagon will be better for the baby. You can feed and change her whenever you need to. The straw should make you both more comfortable."

"Well, if you are sure."

"And I have a surprise for you." He turned to look up the path.

"A surprise?" Louisa glanced in that direction and wondered what the surprise would be. A bath would be welcome, as would a change of clothing or a comfortable carriage, but she knew she was being foolish.

"Ahh, yes, here she comes now."

"She?" Louisa turned toward the din of crashing and crackling brush. "What is this surprise? It sounds like a herd of cattle."

"She is a little awkward but I feel sure—"

A short, very round woman emerged from the woods and stood surveying William and Louisa from under thick brows lowered across eyes that flashed with anger.

She put a fist on each broad hip and glowered at the pair.

"I'm here," she said in a loud, fierce voice that had the musicality of hoofbeats.

"Lady Louisa, I'd like you to meet Mrs. Fallworth."

"Titania." The little woman threw shaggy dark hair back with a toss of her head and glowered at them, as if challenging them to laugh at her name. "My mother saw a play once."

"A lovely name." Louisa nodded and smiled. "Unusual to find in the English countryside but lovely, Titania."

"This," he gestured toward Louisa, "is Lady Louisa."

"So pleased to make your acquaintance," Louisa smiled at the irate round woman.

Titania glared back and forth, from Louisa to William, eyes narrow. She held a small sack which she threw into the back of the cart and followed in with a crash.

"What is the reason for Titania?" Louisa whispered to William.

"She's a wet nurse, which Beatrice needs. She seems clean. She lives at the farm where I found the food and bought the horse. Seems her daughter is ready to be weaned, and Titania's mother will take care of her."

"She doesn't look happy about leaving her child."

"No, but I offered her husband more than he could earn from his harvest in years. As chaperone, she will also add a bit of regularity to your situation."

"Thank you for your thoughtfulness."

Beatrice's loud cries announced that the baby had awakened. Louisa went to the back of the wagon to sing to Bea as she changed the baby. "This is Bea," she said to Titania as she handed her the baby. "The viscount tells me you're a wet nurse."

The young woman opened her dress and allowed the baby to nurse while Louisa slowly climbed into the back.

William snapped the reins and called, "Let's go, Black." They departed slowly.

The wagon was far more comfortable than riding. Louisa spread her sore legs apart and leaned against the side of the vehicle to watch William drive. Next to her, she'd placed a piece of her torn riding habit and put the baby on it to sleep when Titania had finished nursing. The wet nurse dozed in the back, snoring more loudly than a brigade of Hussars.

William's unmentionables did indeed protect her legs from rubbing each other. She also discovered that, if she sat with her knees pointed away from each other she was much more comfortable. What a hoyden she was becoming! She pulled the skirt to cover her unladylike position and sat up straight.

"Are we going to Bury-Saint-Edmund now?" she asked after a few comfortable minutes of rocking along in the old wagon.

"I hope so. I'm making a wide circle in the hope of

eluding our pursuers. We should come out northeast of there."

"Good. That will be close to Mopsie's home. Will sheltering Bea be dangerous for Mopsie?"

"I think not. The name of the former nurse of Arnold's wife is not exactly a well known piece of information."

If he had had nothing on his mind, William would have enjoyed the scenery. Instead, as he passed the hedgerows, tilled fields and grazing sheep, he kept his eyes on the road, nervous about the length of time this escape was taking. Blast it! Traveling in this wagon slowed them down so much he was surprised when, with every turn in the road, they did not run right into the traitors.

Even riding in a wagon couldn't be good for Beatrice. The child was so young. If Bea had to travel, this was probably better than racketing around the countryside in his arms, but she needed to be in a crib.

"Please tell me again about Bea." Louisa's question interrupted his thoughts. "You say her father is a spy? How do you and my brother-in-law know him?"

He looked over his shoulder at the sleeping Titania before he continued. "We were together at Cambridge. He's a friend. Not a peer but a gentleman, wealthy and patriotic. His mother was an emigré so he speaks flawless French. None of us knew his wife was increasing when he left for France. He's sent us a great deal of information and will return shortly with even more. The French don't know where he is, but someone found out about Bea. I don't know how," he added before Louisa could ask. "And I don't know who told them."

He guided the horse around a rough spot in the road before he continued. "We thought we had taken care of things well. We didn't know there were spies in the office, but that is the only way they could have gotten the information. We fear they will get the baby and threaten to kill her unless our friend tells the traitors what he knows and the identity of those who worked with him in France. For himself, he'd sooner die, but he could not give up his own daughter. How much can we ask of a man?"

"You said the spies do not know Margaret is Bea's mother."

"No, they know very little, only where the baby was before we took her to Arnold's estate. Then, somehow, they discovered that location too."

When the baby began to whimper, William looked down between them. "Is she all right?"

Louisa nodded. For a moment, he looked at her. Her wrinkled straw-covered skirt was tucked modestly over her legs. She was sitting board-straight against the side of the wagon, her hair pulled back in a disintegrating braid with two broken feathers. Her gloves were dirty although white patches showed through. In spite of the dirt, her attitude was of a woman riding an open carriage in the park at the fashionable hour of five o'clock.

When he burst out laughing, she looked at him as if he was a toad or lizard.

"I'm sorry." But he couldn't explain to her why he'd laughed. She'd be so insulted she'd probably sniff and read him a lecture. "The whole adventure is so unbelievable." He faced forward again and slapped the reins. The wagon jerked ahead.

After almost an hour of silence, William's voice broke into Louisa's contemplation. "Tell me about your family. How many nephews and nieces do you have?"

"Ten. Isn't that amazing? And I don't know how it happened."

"You don't know how your ten nephews and nieces were conceived? You may wish to speak with your sisters."

"No, no, you terrible man. That's not at all what I mean!"

"Then, what do you mean?"

"What I really don't understand is how did I end up a maiden aunt? One day I was a normal debutante, enjoying fetes and Venetian breakfasts, and the next my brothers and sisters were married and I had an increasing number of nieces and nephews to visit."

"Do you regret it?"

"Of course not. I have a wonderful, loving family."

"But still, I'm sure there were men who were interested in you, who proposed. Certainly you had a chance to marry. Do you not regret not having married?"

She repeated, "Of course not. I have a wonderful family and I adore my nephews and nieces."

"Don't you ever think of seeking pleasure for yourself?"

"Being with my family is what I most enjoy," she said with a note of finality.

"Well, it's obvious you don't want to continue that conversation," he said with a smile. "Tell me, what is so exceptional about your nieces and nephews?"

This started her on a narrative about her family until Beatrice awoke and began to beg for her morning refreshment.

After Titania fed the baby, William stopped the wagon to allow a rest period. Louisa changed the baby's cloth while Titania entered the woods with the usual cacophony as she seemed to push trees aside and trample small animals.

"How does a person make such sounds?" Louisa wondered aloud. "I have heard about elephants in India, but I do not believe they could make nearly so much noise."

"An interesting comparison, Louisa. I have never thought about a herd of elephants crashing through Essex."

When Titania rumbled back through the trees, William said, "I believe you are right. It wouldn't sound much different."

Louisa laughed with him. "Do you want me to drive the wagon this afternoon? I'm very good at it." She struggled to climb over the side of the cart and stand on the grass.

"I'm sure you are but thank you, I'm fine. I'm going to let the horse have lunch too." He loosened all the horses, took them to drink then tied them loosely to a tree to allow them to graze. He offered his arm to support Louisa to the clearing where they ate thick slices of bread and some of the cheese Titania brought with her. After too short a time, he tied the horses to the wagon and hitched Black up. Once Louisa, Titania and Bea were settled in the cart, he jumped on the seat and slapped the reins. The large horse started to move slowly.

An hour later, Louisa continued to study the road that stretched out behind them as the wagon swayed up a hill. "William, there are some horsemen coming." She pointed behind them.

William stopped the wagon and turned to look.

Louisa stood, not even noticing pain in her legs. Way back down at the bottom of the long hill, she could barely make out three figures but they were coming fast. She fell down in the wagonbed when William started the horse quickly. "What do you think? Is it the spies chasing us?"

"It could be. We cannot wait to find out." His eyes searched the thick trees on each side of the road.

"This looks like a good place." He pulled the cart

through a narrow opening and drove parallel to the road so the wagon was screened from view by the tall thick brush.

Without a word, he jumped from the seat and ran to the back of the wagon, grabbed the saddle and threw it on Charger's back. "I'm going to lead them away from Bea. You stay here until they're long past."

"But—"

"Give me enough time to get far ahead of you before you leave. I'll lead them away from Essex. Remember, you must get the baby to your nurse's home and get back to tell Arnold where she is." He looked at her with eyes that were dark and challenging. "Forget about me. You have to keep her safe. You know how important this is for our country. Can you do this?"

"Of course I can. I'll take care of her." She climbed onto the seat of the wagon and took the reins.

"Here's some money." He handed her some coins which she tied up in a handkerchief and pushed up the sleeve of her habit. He then mounted Charger and rode him through the brush onto the road, waiting until they could hear the hoofbeats of the three men behind them before he kicked the stallion. Louisa listened to him race off.

Seconds passed. The sounds of the horses came nearer. Louisa took a deep breath and held it until they went on past, but they didn't. The men pulled their mounts to a stop only a few feet from where the cart was barely concealed by the thin screen of branches.

"Well, Green, what do you think?" a man asked, his voice deep and commanding.

"I saw only one horse. Do you think he has the child?"

"He might. What else do we know?" a man who spoke with a slight French accent asked. "What choice do we have but to follow him?"

There was a moment of silence. As she realized how close she was to the men hunting for Bea, Louisa felt her breath catch in her chest.

Why didn't the men ride on? Sitting as still as she could, and certain the villains on the other side of the trees were able to hear her slightest motion, she silently exhaled, took in another breath and held it. Looking up, she could see the outlines of the men through the leaves. Why hadn't they chosen a better hiding place for the wagon? she cursed silently. Of course, they'd thought the men would ride on, in pursuit of William.

From behind her came a rustle in the straw. Louisa turned slowly on the seat, careful not to allow it to creak but, in spite of her caution, she heard a soft squeak and froze in position until she realized the men hadn't heard it. What she saw over her shoulder made her bite her lip. Bea was waking up. In a moment, she would begin to scream for her dinner.

Louisa lifted her glance to Titania. The wet nurse's eyes were wide and her lips were clenched together as she looked at the baby. Both women were too far away from Bea to pick her up without making the straw rustle. Louisa held her breath and whispered, "Oh, please, God."

"I guess we have no choice but to follow the rider. We have no other clues," the one called Green said. "I recognize Woodstone's horse. But I think this is too great a coincidence, that he'd ride out in front of us. He's trying to lead us away from something."

Louisa tried to look through the screen of leaves and found a small opening. She flinched when she realized that she could see the eyes of one of the men. They were cold and icy gray. Could he see her? Louisa again held still.

"*Allons-y,*" said the man with the accent. "Let us go."

Oh, yes, Louisa thought. *Go! Now!*

"I don't know," Green said. "Where's the woman they said went with him and the baby?"

How did he know that? Before she considered what the words meant, she was distracted by a whimper. Bea's eyes were open and she was looking around. Her tiny fingers were starting to curl into fists. Then she took a deep breath. Louisa knew what would be next. *Oh, sweet baby, please don't cry.*

"Etienne, where do you think they are?" Green said.

"We don't have much choice but to follow the bait and hope he'll lead us back to the brat."

"Besides, the others will be searching for the woman and the baby. We might as well follow his trail," said the man with the deep voice. "We will kill them when we find all of them—except the baby."

A tremor went through Louisa at the man's calm acceptance of the need for Titania's and her deaths. Behind her, she could hear the baby rustling in the straw and, on the road, the movement of the horses. She prayed the noise of the animals would hide the sounds of Bea's movements.

"Of course," said the man called Etienne.

With a little cough, Bea emptied her lungs and opened her mouth wide to take another deep breath.

"We're wasting time here. Let's go!"

Saying a prayer of thanks that the sound of the horses thundering off were louder than Bea's cries, Louisa slumped down in the seat. Titania gathered the baby in one arm while she opened her dress and allowed the infant to nurse. When the sound of the chase faded away, Louisa turned to Titania, whose eyes were wide with terror.

"We should have told you, Titania." She was overwhelmed by shame for dashing into this escapade and putting others, innocent others like Titania, in jeopardy. She was no different from William. "I'm sorry we didn't. There are some men who want Beatrice. They want to hurt her father through her. We're trying to hide her where they won't find her."

"They want to kill me?" Titania's body shivered with fear.

"I'm sure the viscount will distract the men," Louisa continued although she wasn't at all certain. What had that man said? That there were others who also searched for them? "I know we'll be safe," she lied. "We just have to be careful."

"Yes, my lady," Titania said with a trembling voice.

Louisa turned back around and waited for almost an hour before pulling out of the woods. As she drove, she looked down at her hands which were encased in badly stained gloves. How ridiculous she must look in her bedraggled hat and tattered riding habit. Anyone would know that she wasn't a simple country lass driving the wagon to market with her cousin and child in the back. Her appearance could put all three of them in danger.

She looked around to where Bea slept and the wet nurse wore a wary look. People would assume Titania and Bea were mother and daughter, but who was the disreputable gentlewoman driving the cart? She took off her hat and tossed it into the woods, then stripped off the gloves which followed the hat.

Her hair was in great disarray already. She rubbed straw in it and pulled a few more strands loose, but her clothing obviously didn't belong to a simple country miss. Well, there was nothing she could do now except for the gold decorations. She pulled the top button off and tossed it to the side of the road, but the other buttons and the braid were sewn on too tight to come off. For a moment, she cursed the elegant trim that used to please her so and the careful seamstress who had attached it so well. Finished with that ineffective exercise, she rubbed dirt on the bright decorations to dim them. Then she reached behind her for a blanket and draped it over her shoulders. That would have to do.

She sat straight in the seat, lifted her chin and snapped the reins, driving toward Bury-Saint-Edmund with far more confidence than she felt.

Chapter Six

Back roads, country roads, bumpy dirt roads. She took so many roads that day, and they all led northeast. At least, Louisa hoped they led in that direction. Every time she chose a road she thought led east, as if to thwart her it turned west or south. She tried to keep an eye on the sun, but the tracks went through forests so thick she couldn't see it.

In the back of the cart, Bea slept next to Titania. The sound of the woman's snoring threatened to bring down the branches about them, but Bea continued to sleep, deaf to the cacophony. Louisa had started to feel a certain comfort with Titania's loud snores. There was a naturalness about them that helped her stay calm amid the terrifying turn her life had taken.

By midday, Louisa's bottom was sore from her

cramped position on the seat, and her legs ached from the previous day's wounds. She stopped at a farmhouse and bought some cheese and bread to share with Titania.

While she drove, her thoughts turned often to William. Had they caught him? Had they killed him? No, she refused to consider the possibility.

Nothing extraordinary happened that day, unless one counted the curious fact that she was driving an infant and her wet nurse along the roads of rural England. In addition, she, Lady Louisa Walker, wore the tatters of her formerly extremely fashionable riding habit. Were members of London society's finest to see her, they would give her the cut for wearing such rags.

She saw an ox cart on the road and passed a number of workers in fields but encountered no one who looked as if they were hunting for Beatrice.

As the sun began to set and Louisa was searching for a barn in which to spend the night, Titania said in her curious growl, "My uncle lives close."

"He does?" Louisa glanced over her shoulder at Titania. "Can we get something to eat there?"

"We can sleep there." She pointed east. At least it was on the way to their destination.

The house was a small, comfortable cottage in which everyone congregated around the hearth. Titania's relatives, Mr. and Mrs. Durwood and their three children, welcomed Titania. Although they were bewildered that their niece would travel with this unkempt gentlewoman and unknown baby, they embraced Louisa and Bea kindly.

After Mr. Durwood took care of the horses and Titania had fed and put the baby down to sleep, Mrs. Durwood ladled out a delicious stew, rich with vegetables. Louisa devoured it with great relish, too hungry to be embarrassed at her appetite. She used thick, crusty bread to soak up the gravy then sat back with a sigh and rudely dozed in the chair.

When Titania's family placed a straw pallet before the fireplace, Louisa was so exhausted she fell onto it and was asleep almost before Titania settled for the night, and the rest of the family dispersed to the one bedroom and loft.

Louisa awoke in the middle of the night, fear clutching her heart. Wide awake, she sat up, filled with sudden panic and wondering what Lady Louisa Walker was doing here, sleeping on the floor of a tenant farmer's cottage, dashing along unfamiliar roads with a wet nurse who seldom spoke, and attempting to save the life of the daughter of a British spy.

Why wasn't she sleeping in a comfortable bed in one of the lovely suites her family saved for her? Why was she sleeping on the floor next to a woman whose snores caused the furniture to vibrate, and the embers in the fireplace to burst into flame?

I'm not the type of person who likes to dart hither and yon in dirty clothes and sleep on the floor.

Louisa took a deep breath and lay down again. In the

dark, the thought of those cold gray eyes, the steely stare that pierced the screen of leaves separating her from the scoundrel, caused her to sit up again. She'd always considered herself fearless. It was a lowering thought to realize she was not a brave person.

And William. Where was he? Was he alive? Had he drawn the spies away or were they circling back toward Beatrice?

Oh, dear Lord, help me! Help us all. Having turned her cares over to God, she took a deep breath, and turned over on the thin pallet to fall into a dreamless sleep.

Louisa awoke surrounded by the farmer's family preparing to go out into the field. As she pulled the pallet out of the way, she saw Titania feeding Bea while Mrs. Durwood ladled out bowls of hot gruel that they dipped up with toast. Louisa had never seen gruel before nor had she realized toast could be eaten without marmalade, but she found everything delicious. She washed it all down with weak tea, and was ready to go when Mrs. Durwood handed her a dress.

"My niece Titania told us what you are doing, how you're trying to save the country. I think you might look more like us if you wore this." Mrs. Durwood pointed toward the bedroom door. "You can put it on in there."

"Do you have salve or ointment?" Louisa asked Mrs. Durwood. "I have some sores on my legs." She took the pottery jar her hostess handed to her into the bedroom.

After slipping off her torn and filthy habit, Louisa allowed William's unmentionables to drop to the floor. She unwrapped the strips and rubbed the tender skin with the salve, then pulled the trousers back up and tied them around her waist. Her legs were still too raw to leave the dirty garment behind.

The dress was of well-worn cotton. Louisa guessed it had started life dark blue but had faded from wear and the washings which had also made it soft. When she put the dress on, it hung from her shoulders, which was fine. It made her look different, transformed her into a country woman.

Nothing could be done with her hair. It curled riotously around her head, and she had lost the last pin the previous day. After tearing a strip of ragged lace from her chemise, Louisa braided her hair loosely and tied it behind her.

She touched her nose. It was burned, probably red and shiny. She'd soon have freckles as she'd had as a carefree child. She laughed. Gone was Lady Louisa. In her place was someone she recognized from years ago and had liked back then. How had she changed from the carefree girl to the maiden aunt? She knew. Yes, she knew what had happened to the young Louisa. Shrugging, she put away those thoughts. When running from French spies, one did not have time for introspection.

Louisa took the habit into the other room and gave it

to Mrs. Durwood. "There are gold buttons on here. Please, take them off and use them if you need to."

"No." Mrs. Durwood sat down with the habit and a knife. "You may need them to take care of that baby." She sliced the decorations off and handed them to her.

"Thank you." Louisa wrapped them in the handkerchief with William's coins. "Would you throw this away?" She gestured toward the habit.

"Oh, no," Mrs. Durwood said, rubbing her hand across the thick fabric of the full skirt as if it was the finest velvet. "It's beautiful. You don't want it?"

"No, you may have it. What will you do with it?"

"Oh, I'll brush and clean it. It will make such a nice jacket for my son and a wonderful pair of trousers for Mr. Durwood." She looked up. "Please keep that baby safe."

"I will. Thank you."

"We'll keep your riding horse here, Lady Louisa," Mr. Durwood said. "No need for her to plod around the countryside tied to the back of that wagon. She'll give you away."

While Titania made her final preparations and bid her relations farewell, Louisa went to the road where the boys had hitched the heavy horse to the cart.

"We put new traces on the black horse too," Mr. Durwood said. "Those others were going to wear through on you."

"Thank you, thank all of you."

"Now, if you want to go toward Bury, take this road until you come to a good, smooth road. Go east. You'll get there by this evening. We have cousins on the way who'll help you. Titania knows where they live."

"I don't know how I can thank you." She placed Bea on her blanket on the straw and climbed into the seat with less pain than the day before. When Titania had ensconced herself in the back, Louisa snapped the reins. With a gentle step, Black took off and settled into his slow but steady pace.

The day was like the previous one. The gentle rocking of the wagon lulled Bea and Titania to sleep. They drove by high hedgerows and past farmland. When they passed through a tiny village, Titania shouted, "That's Wimberton!"

It was still early morning when Louisa heard horses coming toward her fast. She said, "Cover Bea," to the wet nurse.

Louisa hunched over, dropped her head down between her shoulders, and kept her eyes on Black's back. When she looked quickly behind her, she saw Titania had pulled Bea next to her and put the blanket over the baby and her lap.

Louisa kept the horse at his regular amble. Within seconds, she saw William riding Charger toward her at top speed. Their eyes met for a second, both expressing surprise but giving no other sign of recognition. When he had passed, without even considering the conse-quences, she tugged on the reins to slow the cart so it blocked the road. On the sides of the narrow track were thick thorny bushes so the three men who rounded the corner only seconds behind William had to pull up.

"Move the wagon!" one of the men yelled. The three men moved their horses back and forth, looking for a way to get around the obstacle.

Louisa sawed on the reins, pretending to straighten the wagon. Because she didn't know any of these men, she doubted they would recognize her, but she still kept her head down.

"Woman, get that wagon out of the way!" one of them said.

Another man slapped Black with his whip and raised it toward Louisa who cowered with her arm over her face. She fumbled with the reins to move Black to the center of the road just as the last man rode past.

What was she going to do? She had to get Bea to a safe place, but those men were going to kill William.

She couldn't sacrifice his life to keep Beatrice safe. Oh, he'd told her to forget him, but she wouldn't allow William to die. She had to do something but what? And how could she keep Bea and Titania safe?

"I want to go home!" Titania sobbed. "I don't want to stay out here with the spies." Her howls caused the trees above them to shower the cart with leaves.

"I'll take you back home. Just be quiet for a moment."

The yowls became whimpers.

"I'm looking for a place to turn around," she

explained as Titania's screeches began anew. When she found a broad place in the road, she turned the wagon in a wide arc and made the turn with little space to spare. "Thank goodness," she murmured. She had no idea how to back a horse.

Headed back in the direction they'd come, the direction in which the men had disappeared, Louisa searched the road and the fields on each side. She drove for miles through settling dust until she could no longer guess where William might have gone.

"Wimberton," Titania said.

"What?"

"There's a constable in Wimberton, the village we went through earlier. He might help you. Then you can take me back to my aunt and uncle."

So Louisa backtracked to Wimberton.

It was not much of a town, she thought when they arrived. Not even a church, just a few stores and houses and a small wooden building in front of which the three men that had been chasing William had tied their horses beside Charger.

"That's it." Titania pointed to the building. "That's the parish constable's."

Louisa pulled the wagon to a stop a short distance from the horses, jumped out, and walked to the window of the office, keeping low and to the side so those inside couldn't see her. From the side of the window, she could see five men. Four of them had their backs to the window. Three of the men she'd seen before, the ones who had chased William. One was tall; one was short and round; the third was balding.

William sat and watched the fifth man, who stood on the other side of a small table from him. Obviously the constable.

"This man is a traitor," the tall man said. "We have to take him back to London." He handed the constable a sheaf of papers. "I have the legal right to escort the viscount back to London."

"Let's not hurry." The constable rustled the papers and sat at the desk. "I'll need to study these."

Louisa raced back to the wagon, her mind churning.

"We're going back to the farm," Louisa said when she feared Titania was about to bawl and alert the men to their presence.

While she drove back to the Durwoods' farm, Louisa tried to come up with a plan to save William. What was she going to do?

"Dear Lord, help me!" she prayed, amazed she'd become so familiar with the Deity lately. A staunch member of the Church of England, she usually met Him only during Sunday services, but in the last few days, she'd found Him to be most helpful.

As Louisa drove into the yard of the Durwoods' farm, Titania said, "Look, that's my favorite cousin." With a resounding crash, she jumped off the wagon and walked to a sturdy dark-haired boy who stood with Mr. Durwood.

A scheme to rescue William started to form when

she saw the child. It was ridiculous, like the adventure books she read to her nephews, but she had to do something before those men carried William away. She began planning details, then decided there was no time. She would have to set the scheme in motion and hope it would work.

"What are you doing here?" Mrs. Durwood rushed out of the house. "Are you hurt?"

Louisa let herself down the side of the wagon and walked to the family. "Titania wanted to come home," Louisa explained.

"Oh, Auntie, I was so frightened. There were murderers chasing us." Her sobs caused the door of the house to fly open. "I don't want to ride in the wagon anymore."

"Of course you may stay, both of you." Mrs. Durwood patted Titania's shoulder before she turned to Louisa. "Will you spend the night with us again?"

"Thank you, I cannot. I have something I must do." She looked at the boy who looked to be about ten years old.

"My lady, this is my nephew Donald," Mr. Durwood began when he saw Louisa look at him. "He just arrived for a visit. First time we've seen him in years."

"No one in Wimberton knows Donald?" Louisa asked.

"No, no," Mrs. Durwood answered. "He hasn't visited us since he was four or five."

"As you know, we are trying to save the baby."

Louisa nodded toward the cart where Bea slept. "And a most courageous gentleman. I have a plan but I need to borrow Donald."

The family turned and looked at her, eyes wide.

"You want to borrow Donald?" Titania asked blankly.

"The viscount is in the constable's office, and I fear the French traitors will try to carry him off. I need to try to get him away from them. I have a plan."

"Is this for the King?" Mr. Durwood asked.

"Yes, it is. For crown and country."

"You can believe her," Titania said. "We've been driving all over, trying to help the King."

"Then I don't have a choice." Donald stood straighter and turned toward Louisa. "What must I do?"

"Mr. and Mrs. Durwood?"

"Is there any danger?" Mrs. Durwood asked.

"I believe not. I'll protect him. Perhaps you could come to Wimberton to watch over him, Mr. Durwood?"

The farmer nodded. "What else can we do, my lady?"

"Can you find some other men and bring them to the constable's office? If we all work together, I believe I can get the viscount away and keep Donald safe."

Louisa started back to the wagon, then turned when she suddenly realized that she was putting even more people at risk. "No, I'm sorry. I was wrong. There may be danger, and I cannot put another child at peril. I will do this on my own."

"But, my lady, this is about spies," Titania said.

"French spies?" Mrs. Durwood asked.

"Yes, but I cannot tell you more."

"My lady, we have to help you," Mr. Durwood said. "None of us will be safe if those spies win. There's far more danger for Donald and all of us if we let the French win."

"I must stress the risk involved."

"Are you saying that only the nobility is patriotic? That we common folk cannot help against the French?" Mr. Durwood bit off his words and glared at Louisa.

"Not at all, but the boy—"

"I'll keep an eye on him, and all my friends will be there. Just give me a time to get them together." Mr. Durwood turned to go back to the stable. "If I could ride your horse, it won't take much time." He ran back to saddle Bess when Louisa nodded.

Louisa turned to Mrs. Durwood and Titania. "Will you take care of Bea while I'm gone?"

"Of course, my lady," Mrs. Durwood said. "We will do what we must do for our country."

"Donald, let me tell you what you'll need to do," Louisa explained as the two drove toward Wimberton. "If anything happens to me, take Bea to Longtrees. It's an estate in Essex. My sister lives there, and she'll know what to do." She pressed some coins in his hand.

They arrived in Wimberton as the constable left the building. The three men pushed William ahead of them.

After Louisa and Donald got out of the wagon, she pointed to William.

"Papa!" Donald ran to him and threw himself at his feet, sobbing. "Papa! Where have you been?"

William jumped away from the child, then looked up to see Louisa. His eyes grew angry and he turned away from her as he attempted to shake loose the child who clung to his boots.

Louisa dashed to William and put her arms around his neck. "Just be quiet. I have a plan," she whispered to William, then began to sob. "Chester, Chester, how could you leave us again?" She attempted to imitate the speech of the Durwoods, a little broad and not pronounced precisely.

"You know this man?" the constable asked.

"Of course I know him." Louisa let go of the viscount and turned toward the constable. "He is my husband, Chester Boggs."

"What?" The bald man looked at her as if she was henwitted. "You're daft, woman. This is William of Woodstone."

"Argh, Chester, you didn't tell them that, did you?"

William nodded, dropping his head so his chin lay on his chest.

"Excuse me, missus," the constable said, "but he doesn't sound like a Chester Boggs. He talks like gentry."

"Oh Chester, you fooled them, didn't you?"

William continued to study his shoes.

"Look at his clothes." Louisa gestured toward the dirty and torn shirt and stained unmentionables. "Would a noble wear filthy rags? Would a viscount have bugs in his hair?" She pulled a small insect from his head. "Would a noble smell like he does?" She wrinkled her nose.

"No, missus, but he talks like nobility. These men say they are charged with bringing him back to London for treason."

Louisa glared at the constable. "You're not saying these men from London know my husband better than I do, are you?"

The constable took a step back. "No, Mrs. Boggs."

"He's a traitor, miss," the tall man said. "You're mistaken or daft."

"Oh Chester, aren't you ashamed of yourself?" Louisa put her hands on her hips and shook her head. William attempted to look even more abashed.

"Papa, Papa!" Donald continued to sob at his father's feet.

"How could you tell such tales? How could you leave little Chester and your darling wife?"

"I tell you," another of the men said, "that is Woodstone."

As Louisa twisted to look at him, her hair swirled around her face, and the dress twisted around her waist. "What are you trying to do? Take a husband away from his wife and son? How could you do that? How could an Englishman break up a family?"

By this time, a group of men led by Mr. Durwood began to converge on the street. "Here! Here!" they shouted.

"You're not . . ."—Louisa leaned forward and scrutinized the three spies—"You're not *frogs* are you?"

The crowd began to murmur angrily.

"I've heard those Frenchies are trying to bring our country down by breaking up our families!" she shouted to the crowd.

The men grumbled and moved closer.

"No, miss," said the bald pursuer. "We're here on orders from the Home Office to bring this man in."

"What would the Home Office want with Chester Boggs?" Louisa glared at them.

"We don't want Chester Boggs!" said the short spy.

"Good. Come along, Chester." Louisa took his arm. "Let's go, little Chester."

"Wait a minute!" the first man explained. "That *is* Woodstone, and we're supposed to take him in."

"This is my husband!" Louisa shouted. *Oh my,* she thought to her amazement, *this is fun.*

"Mrs. Boggs," the constable interrupted. "The man does look and talk more like a viscount than a Chester Boggs."

Louisa bristled. "What does that mean? Are you saying a spoiled nobleman is better than one of God's British farmers?"

"No, not at all, Mrs. Boggs." The constable took another step backwards.

"Are you saying," she demanded as she strode toward the constable and he again backed away, "I don't know my own husband?"

"Mrs. Boggs, he didn't deny being the viscount. He just asked me to escort him back to London instead of these three."

"Oh Chester, I'm going to have to tell them." She shook her head in sorrow as she looked at William. He nodded at her.

"Go ahead, Martha," he said in a choked voice.

"The truth of it is—my husband is daft." She patted his arm. "There, I hoped I wouldn't have to tell you here, out in front of everyone, but that's what it is. Poor man is daft. Served in the Army under a fine nobleman, got a wound in the head, and has never been the same since."

"Ohh, poor man!" The crowd had grown as more men and a few women joined it.

"Aye." Louisa turned toward them. "Gave everything for his country. A hero, and now these men want to take him. No telling what they'll do to him, him who suffered for his country."

"No telling," the growing crowd repeated.

"He's daft, Mrs. Boggs?" the constable asked.

"Thinks he's the nobleman who commanded his division. Talks like him and acts like him. Tries to dress like him, too, but we can't buy new clothes. Look at his face. Would a noble run around dirty and unshaved like that?"

"Is that true?" The constable turned toward William who didn't answer but continued to look down at his feet. "Is that true?" the constable said more loudly.

William shrugged and looked confused, rubbing his lightly bearded cheeks.

"You poor woman," the constable said. "And you stay with him. You're a flower of British womanhood."

"Oh, yes, he's still my dear husband and I take care of him. Of course, there are times . . . he twitches, you see."

William's head jerked up. He glared at her with a flash of hostility.

"Yes, he does," Louisa said. "That's disgusting but the poor man tries not to."

"He twitches?" the constable asked.

"Yes, poor dolt." Louisa patted William's head. "But I love him."

"Ahh," the crowd sighed.

"Who are you?" the fat pursuer demanded.

Haughtily, Louisa answered, "I'm Mrs. Chester Boggs." She glared at the three men. "I would like to know who are you? Why do you want to kidnap a woman's husband and a boy's father?"

"Papa!" cried Donald when Louisa nudged him with her foot.

"We've been sent from London to bring back the Viscount Woodstone for treason. This man is not your husband. He's the viscount," the tall man said.

"How can you say that? Does the viscount twitch?"

Louisa gave William a hard poke in the ribs which was rewarded by another glance of antipathy. "My husband can hardly pass ten minutes without twitching." She shot him a demanding look.

William gave a demented laugh and began to twitch. He started shivering from his scuffed boots, up his legs covered with filthy and tattered unmentionables, to his shoulders covered in the rags of his shirt until the motion reached his head where it stopped.

"Look at the poor fellow," Louisa said. "Does that look like your nobleman?"

"We were told to bring him back," the fat man repeated.

"And drools, poor man." Louisa sighed. "When he's really upset, he drools." She looked at William. "Drools all the time, when he's not twitching."

William flashed a look of such antagonism that she feared she'd gone too far. He gave another deranged laugh, then moved closer to Louisa. "I will not drool," he whispered.

"Does he look like a duke or whatever you thought he was?" She picked up the grubby hem of her skirt and wiped his chin.

The three men looked at each other. "No," said the tall one slowly. "It looks like a daft man dressed up to look like a noble. But tell me, then, ma'am, why he was trying so hard to get away from us and where did he get this horse?" He gestured toward Charger who was grazing on the side of the street.

"I'm thinking he ran because you chased him."

"Right!" the crowd muttered. "Poor man."

"And we traded for the horse. A man and a woman came by yesterday with a baby. I gave them some of our clothes. They took off in a cart pulled by one of our old horses. We were keeping that horse." She pointed at Charger. "We were keeping that horse until they came for it. I should have known Chester would see him and decide it was his, thinking himself nobility. Poor, darling, crazy man." She shook her head. "There, there." She patted his shoulder. "Don't worry. We'll go home."

"Let the poor, daft fellow go!" Mr. Durwood shouted. When more men repeated the words and the angry crowd edged forward, chanting, the three men looked around them, uncomfortable.

"Well, gentlemen, I don't think this poor creature is your viscount," the constable said.

"No, I don't either," said the tall spy. "Thank you, constable, for your help. We'd better get on our way."

"Come home with us, dear. We'll let you rest." Louisa allowed William to lean against her. He tried to take a step but couldn't move with Donald wrapped around his feet.

"Come, little Chester." Louisa gestured for the child to stand. "We need to take papa home."

"Papa!" Donald leaned against William's side and the viscount put his arm around the child's shoulders.

"Don't forget that man's horse, Chester." At Louisa's scold, William untied Charger and led the horse by the reins.

"Oh, it's so sweet," said a woman in the crowd, dabbing at her eyes. "To see a family back together."

The three men mounted and rode off in the other direction while the Boggs family walked aimlessly down the road.

When the men were out of sight, William turned to Louisa and said, "What in the world were you doing? There was too much danger for you. Of all the ridiculous—"

"It worked, didn't it, Chester?"

"It worked, at least for a short while. We'd better get on the road because, once they think about it, they're going to come back for another look and bring more men with them."

"You twitch very well, Chester."

"One day, Miss Prim—" He stopped and looked at her, his voice suddenly and unexpectedly softening. "You don't look like Miss Prim anymore."

"It's difficult to look prim driving around in an open cart or rescuing you from three scoundrels." She struggled with her features, attempting to arrange them into a proper expression.

"It's not an adventure, Louisa. We could all die."

"Of course I know that, William, but you men always make adventures from the most perilous situations. You love them and leave us women out." *But the adventure is over,* Louisa thought with a twinge of disappointment. The baby would soon be safe with Mopsie, and she would have to be herself again. Her boring maiden aunt self. She poked at her hair with her fingers in an attempt to bring her fuzzy locks under control until she realized it would take more than her hands to do so.

"Where's the baby?" William asked, interrupting her thoughts.

Chapter Seven

"Here's the baby." Mrs. Durwood rocked Beatrice, touching the baby's soft cheek with hers.

"Could you please keep her?" Louisa asked. "Titania doesn't want to travel so we have no one to nurse her."

"Of course we'll take care of her. She'll be safe here." She kissed Beatrice. "She's too young to be traveling in that bumpy wagon. We'll just tell everyone it's Titania's baby."

"It could be dangerous for you," William warned.

"Lady Louisa told us that," Mr. Durwood said. "In this village, we take care of each other. No one will say a word about the baby. The spies won't know where to find her." He looked at Louisa. "Lady Louisa, how you handled those men, it was the cleverest thing I ever saw."

"Thank you for your help. We could not have won if

those men hadn't been afraid of your mob." Louisa took the sleeping baby and gently rubbed a finger down her cheek. "The Durwoods will take good care of her." She looked up at William. "While they care for Bea, we can lead the spies away."

"Louisa, that will put you in great danger." William drew his eyebrows down into a dark V.

"Everything we're doing is dangerous," Louisa answered, hating the word they kept repeating. "But we have found a safe place for Bea. Now we must be decoys to lead the spies away."

"Louisa, you should not be part of this." William took her hand and pulled her away from the Durwoods. "*I* will lead the men away. *You* are to go to the estate of one of your sisters."

"They are looking for a man and a woman. They won't follow you, a man alone."

He didn't answer but continued to stare at her.

"Or perhaps they'll find me, riding alone. That would be far more risk for me than riding with you." When his expression didn't change, Louisa remembered what Mr. Durwood had said. "Do you believe only men are able to sacrifice for their country?"

"Of course not, but this, Louisa, this is very—"

"Dangerous, I know. Haven't I handled the danger? Didn't I get you away from those men?"

"You shouldn't have. You should have taken Bea away while the men were busy with me. That's what I told you to do!"

"Bea is out of harm's way, and you are alive. I believe I did well." She glared at William. "It is nice to be thanked."

"Thank you, Miss Prim and Self-righteous."

"Not very graciously done, but you're welcome."

With a mixture of anger and defeat, William again turned back toward Mrs. Durwood. "Your husband says that you will not suffer from this, but I worry."

"I agree with my husband. No one will know who little Bea is. If something happens, well, we have to do this for our beloved country. This is urgent, isn't it?"

"Yes, Mrs. Durwood, it is." Woodstone twisted his signet ring from his finger. "When it is safe, either Lady Louisa or I will come back for the baby. If we are unable to come, I will send someone with this ring." He handed it to her. After inspecting it, she passed it to her husband who also studied the emblem before he returned it to William.

"A tree and a deer." Mr. Durwood nodded. "We'll recognize that."

William shoved the ring back on his finger and turned to Louisa. "Well, my lady, are you ready to go?"

Louisa stood. She had carefully rebraided her hair and tied it back. With patience, she'd attempted to brush dirt and straw from the blue dress and William's unmentionables but with little success. She'd washed up, scrubbing hard enough that the sunburned skin tingled, but her hands needed far more care than the harsh soap could provide. Her efforts to return to her appearance as Miss Prim were barely successful. Inside, she savored the excitement the coming adventure promised.

"I am ready. Is Bess?"

"She's had a nice rest, my lady. She's frisky and primed to be ridden. I'll put two blankets in a bundle for you." Mr. Durwood left to saddle the horse.

"It's getting cooler. You'll need a wrap." Mrs. Durwood opened a drawer and took out a black wool shawl.

"That's your church shawl," Titania remonstrated.

"It's lovely." Louisa touched the soft wool then handed it back to Mrs. Durwood. "But it's too lovely to ride around the countryside in. Do you have one you wear every day?"

"You're a lady, Lady Louisa. You can't wear my old shawl."

"If we're to fool these spies, I'll look best in your old shawl." She drew out her handkerchief and took a coin.

"No, Lady Louisa. We're proud to help."

Louisa threw the old shawl over her shoulders and walked to the road where William waited with the horses.

"Are you prepared to ride astride again, Louisa?"

"My legs will be fine, thank you. They've had some time to heal." She stopped as her hands reached automatically to pull on gloves that she didn't have. Instead, she reached out to Mrs. Durwood and said, "Bless you."

Then, looking down at the baby Mrs. Durwood held, she said, "We need a baby!"

"What?"

"We need something that looks like a baby so people will remember the man and the woman—and the baby."

Titania ran back into the house quickly and returned with a blanket which she wrapped about a small piece of wood Mr. Durwood handed her, then held it out to Louisa.

"Thank you," Louisa said. "That should deceive them. Good-bye, Titania. Thank you for you help."

"You're welcome, my lady." Her eyes filled with tears. "I'll take good care of little Bea until you come back. Then I can go home to my baby."

Louisa and William mounted their horses and rode off in the opposite direction from the one the men had taken.

"I couldn't believe it when I saw you in the wagon," William said. "Here I was, leading the spies away, and we ran into you. What were you doing? You were supposed to go to Bury." He looked at Louisa, his dark eyes hard and chin set.

"I tried. Every road we took east ended up winding all over."

"Can you imagine how angry I was to see you?"

"You should be glad we got lost. If I hadn't been there, you would have been in a lot of trouble." It was, Louisa reflected, like talking to one of her nephews when he was bothered. She needed to stay patient, talk slowly and clearly, and attempt to keep him on the subject.

"I would have thought of something."

"What?" she asked haughtily. "Oh, never mind. Just tell me what happened. I have some information you should know, but if you're going to be disagreeable, I shan't tell you."

William laughed. "Ahh, Miss Prim is back!" More seriously, he said, "Thank you for coming to my rescue. I cannot imagine how you came up with such an ingenious idea." At her nod of acceptance, he continued. "Nothing happened. I rode around, leading the spies away from you while you were busy *not* going to Bury."

"Well, if you're going to dwell on that, I won't tell you what I heard when we hid in the bushes." Louisa turned her head to the side and scrutinized the trees.

"All right, I'm sorry."

Louisa's head swiveled. "What? Woodstone apologizes?"

"You could accept my apology graciously."

"You are right. Thank you." Louisa smiled. "When you left us, the three men who were chasing us stopped and had a conversation next to where we were hiding."

"They stopped next to the wagon?" William looked at her intently. "Could you see them? What did they say?"

"I couldn't see much so I'd never recognize their faces, but I heard them clearly. They said other men are looking for Bea all over, and they would kill you and me if they found us."

He looked at Louisa. "I'm sorry to have pulled you into this. I can face death myself but to put you in peril—"

"You had no other choice."

"No, I didn't. What can you tell me about the men?"

"One was called Green."

"That doesn't surprise me. We've heard of him but nothing good. Who else?"

"One of them had a French accent. They called him Etienne."

"Ahh." William scowled. "Etienne D'Estange, back in England. This *is* very important to them."

"The third one . . ." Louisa stopped and thought. "The third man spoke with a deep voice and gave orders. When he looked through the leaves, he didn't see me, but I saw his eyes. I don't believe I'll ever forget them. They were gray and cold." She shivered. "Does that help?"

"It convinces me that Green isn't the leader. I wonder if this man with the gray eyes is with the Home Office? Would you recognize him?"

"Not his face, but I'll remember his eyes and his voice for the rest of my life."

William said nothing and seemed to be in deep thought.

After a pause, Louisa asked, "How long do we have to ride?"

"A day or two should be enough."

"If the traitors find us, won't they notice we're no longer in a wagon and that you have your horse back from poor Chester Boggs?"

"We can only hope there will be enough conflicting and odd stories being reported about us that those details will not be as obvious to them as they are to us."

They rode for another mile before William said, "Louisa, should anything happen to us, should the spies find us, you must get away. I'll fight them as long as I can, but you must escape and get to London. Do you understand?"

"Of course, William."

He looked at his accomplice. There was an air of expectancy about her, a sparkle that had been lacking before. Her hair was as neat and tidy as she could arrange it, although it had begun to straggle despite Louisa's numerous pokes to keep it straight. She sat the horse comfortably, her legs demurely covered by the skirt of the dress, at least as far as the material stretched. At her knees, the faded blue garment stopped and his trousers covered her to the ankles. In the sunlight that filtered through the leaves overhead, her nose shone pink, and freckles were scattered across it. He wanted to touch them. He wanted to kiss them.

Devil a bit! Where had that thought come from? They were out here, alone. She was completely defenseless. On top of that, he'd promised not to touch her and here he was, wanting to kiss her like a lovesick young pup—well, more like a seasoned rake which Louisa did not deserve at all.

Then Louisa interrupted his thoughts. "Milk," she said. She held out the bundle that was supposed to be the baby. "You need to stop for milk for the baby."

"Louisa, our little bundle doesn't need milk."

"I know that. But you want people to remember us, in case someone asks about a man and a woman and a baby." Louisa pointed. "There's a farm ahead."

"Good idea. Can you cry like a baby?" At her nod, he continued. "Let us hear little whimpers, like a hungry baby."

William dismounted and Louisa turned away from the farmhouse. When William began to talk, she started to cry.

"How did I do?" she asked when William returned with a cup of milk and some food.

"Loudest baby I've ever heard. The farmer's wife said she thinks little Bea has colic, and you're not taking care of her correctly. She lectured me about what a bad mother you are." He handed some of the milk to Louisa to drink then poured the rest on the grass and remounted the horse.

"I hope you told her I'm a marvelous mother."

"Why? She'll remember a terrible mother who allows her child to wail." He smiled at her. "You can't be comfortable holding the baby. Let me have it." He reached out, took the bundle, and balanced it across the front of the saddle.

"What a terrible parent you are!"

He reached into the package of food he'd bought from the farmer. "Here's some bread and cheese. Do you want some?"

"Can we stop? I hate to eat cheese on a horse. It's messy. My hands get all sticky and there's no place to wash."

"Ahh, still Miss Prim." He laughed.

"Did you think I'd changed completely?"

"Of course not." He pulled the horses to the side of the road. "I see a brook over there. We can dismount and you may eat your cheese in the utmost propriety."

"Oh, yes. Nothing is more proper than eating cheese alone with a man somewhere in England with no chaperone."

Louisa dismounted and led Bess toward the brook. For a moment, William watched her, wondering about the emotion growing in him, wondering about the certainty that his regard had grown far beyond what one felt for a comrade. He shook his head, attempting to force any tenderness away before he joined her.

"I have to admit one thing," he said as he settled on a log next to her. "I do admire your pluck and ingenuity." He took a bite of the bread. "When you were Mrs. Chester Boggs, how did you think of that idiotic twitching?"

"My nephews have a favorite story I've read to them many times. It involves a great deal of twitching and drooling and other disgusting actions." She chuckled at him, her eyes twinkling with mirth. "Are you still upset about it?"

"I don't believe I've ever seen *you* twitching."

"No,"—she shook her head, still teasing—"you haven't but that doesn't mean I've never done anything embarrassing. During my first season—"

"Tell me about your first season."

She turned toward him, surprised. "Why would you want to know about that?" Her back straightened, and she brushed back loose curls.

For a moment he studied her, looking into eyes that looked violet in the shade. He thought how easy it would be to allow them to enchant him.

"I remember you at seventeen, and I see you now. How could a young woman as lovely as you were not have been inundated by offers of marriage?"

"How did I end up an old maid? Is that what you're asking?"

"Indelicately phrased, not with words *I* would have chosen, but yes."

"Well, if you must know, you were part of it. For a while, I was waiting for you," she stated matter-of-factly.

"Louisa, what we shared wasn't a grand passion. We were very young and had no idea of what love was."

"Well, perhaps you didn't but I loved you dearly. I was devastated when you left me."

"I didn't leave you."

"What? You were gone. I never saw you again until . . . until now."

"Well, I didn't leave you, exactly. Your father invited me to depart after he very correctly pointed out that I was a younger son with no prospects, and you were very young and could not know your mind. He made it very clear that an offer would not be accepted, that you had a season in London coming up, and he expected you to make a brilliant match there."

"What? My father told you to leave?" She considered the words. They should not have surprised her. Her father was protective of his family and as high handed as any man in society. "He had no right to interfere."

"Of course he did. He was your father. And he wasn't interfering. He was taking care of you."

"He could have talked to me. He should have told me."

"What good would that have done? He was right, Louisa. I had nothing to offer you then."

"You had everything I wanted." For a moment her anger almost brought tears of frustration and sorrow. "For years I thought you'd just left. I should have been told."

"Louisa, your father cared for you greatly. He probably thought that was the best way to handle this. He wanted you to marry a man who could supply the best in life for you, as he always had and as I obviously couldn't."

She started to speak but instead turned to watch the hedges along the road and to struggle with her anger. Wisely, William said nothing. After she couldn't guess how long, she finally had to accept what her father had done. She couldn't change things after all this time, and his actions were what most fathers, probably all fathers, would've done.

Now she and William were two older and very different people. It was much too late to worry about the past.

"Besides," William said as she faced the road, "it was probably a fortunate escape for you. I would make a terrible husband."

"Why is that?"

"I am shallow and easily distracted. I put my own desires and interests ahead of those of others."

Louisa stopped nibbling on her cheese. "Oh, that's why you are running all over England to keep a baby safe?"

As if she hadn't spoken, he continued: "I am not loyal nor am I interested in being faithful to one woman, and I do not like children."

"You have taken good care of Bea and I remember you caring greatly for your younger sister."

"Ah, yes, there are two children I care about out of *all* the children on the island. The chances of my appreciating my own are small."

"You paint yourself too black. I don't believe you are that bad."

"Consider yourself lucky for escaping, Louisa." He tore off a piece of bread and handed it to her. "Now, tell me about why you haven't married. Certainly you couldn't have waited for me for eight years."

"No, even I am not such a ninny. I received several offers my first two seasons. To the dismay of my father, I rejected them all because they didn't measure up to you. Of course, at that time of my life, no one could have."

"And then?"

"To be absolutely honest, I don't know exactly what happened." She looked off in the distance as if trying to remember, then turned back to him. "I did truly plan to marry, once I realized you were not coming back. My two older sisters had done very well for themselves. They married titles and fortunes, but I saw my sisters change once they were married."

"How?"

"Lucinda, who is the most intelligent one in our family, suddenly became a complete moron because clever women scared Edward. And Julianna turned into a five-year-old, constantly begging and wheedling for things from Cosden, unable to do anything for herself. I knew men would expect me to behave like a featherbrained ninny. I tried. I made a valiant attempt because I wanted to marry but just couldn't do it."

"It's commendable that you were true to yourself."

She grinned. "Oh yes, I'm sure all your lady friends are intelligent and carry on conversations about politics and laws."

"We are not talking about my lady friends, not that I have any," he answered, suddenly embarrassed that she should speak as if he had a virtual harem. He stroked what was becoming a beard. "Not all men are looking for a brainless idiot to wed."

"Well, all the men I met were. When I was nineteen, I frightened men off in droves! I could *not* act like an idiot. When they found out I preferred to watch Shakespeare than to flirt at the theatre, gossip circulated that I was a bluestocking. On top of that, I didn't simper."

"I cannot imagine you simpering." He barely suppressed a grin.

"I did learn to flirt a little. At least, I can flutter my eyelashes. Let me show you." Thick black lashes covered her beautiful eyes for an instant. "There!" She peeked up at him. "Was that charming?"

It was more than charming. For a moment, he couldn't speak. He cleared his throat and nodded.

Louisa didn't notice his agitation. "By the end of my third season, I was known as an eccentric. No man wants to marry an eccentric. Nonetheless, I wasn't really disappointed."

"Not at all? No regrets?"

"Oh, I would love to have a family but turning myself completely over to a husband and having to spend my life pretending to have no brain at all, an absolute looby, well, I couldn't do it."

"Not even for children?"

"Not even for children." She shook her head. "How can children be happy if their mother is miserable?"

"It happens in many families."

"True, but I didn't want my life or my children's lives to be that way. You see, I remember how much I *used to* love you. It wasn't the memory of you as much as the memory of you I felt then. I was so happy then that I refused to settle for anything less."

"And so, Louisa, you are a romantic," he said in a soft voice.

"And so were you, William. Once."

"But no longer," he said briskly to break the spell Louisa was again casting. "That is another reason why I would make a terrible husband."

"Oh yes. I am so glad you warned me." She laughed.

And with that laugh he realized, as his heart jumped at the sound, that he had not broken the spell at all.

Chapter Eight

"**I** bought a goat." William pointed to the small animal ambling behind him on a piece of rope as he left a farmyard later that afternoon.

"Why would you do that?"

"For the baby."

"But we don't have a—"

"Shh!" William pointed behind him at the couple that watched them from the front of their cottage.

"How wonderful!" Louisa shouted. "Now we don't have to find a farmer to buy milk for the baby." She jiggled the pretend baby and looked down lovingly at its wooden face. "Oh, little Beatrice, now you'll be fed just as soon as you are hungry." Looking up, she waved at the farmer. "Thank you."

As they rode away, Louisa asked, "Where is your coat?"

"I traded it for the goat and gave him a little money. They shan't forget the cabbagehead who paid ten times more than the goat is worth and tossed in his coat as well. The joke will be spread around the area and should leave a wonderful trail for the traitors."

"All right, it was very clever but how fast are we able to ride with her?" Louisa turned around to watch the goat trotting along behind Charger.

"Oh, she'll not slow us down. If we have to escape quickly, I'll just let her go. I haven't grown fond of her yet, although I might, perhaps, in time. I find I have a fondness for a prim and proper female who knows her place."

Louisa rolled her eyes. "But we can't just let her go. She could come to harm wandering around."

"She'll be well taken care of. Some family will find her and be delighted to take her in."

Louisa studied William's face for a moment, then turned away when he noticed her eyes on him.

She'd changed, she reflected. Being close to him no longer sent her into a frenzy. So had he. Just a little, she thought as she peeked at him. His thin face had lost a little of the distrustful look. At times his features softened a bit and the mouth that often seemed so autocratic occasionally curved in a real smile. He looked more like the young William.

His thighs were firm and muscular—she could see them out of the corner of her eye without his being aware of the inspection. Not that she was attracted to the man. However, despite her efforts to stop her eyes, she seemed to have lost control over them. They darted over him, collected information, then came back to look at her hands, folded genteelly across the front of the saddle, an odd contrast to her most unmaidenly thoughts.

In addition to those powerful thighs, her eyes sought a glimpse of the dark hair on his chest. Suddenly, she was filled with a great yearning, a desire so powerful she didn't realize she was capable of such intense emotion.

She tore her eyes from him and kept them on the road. But again, on their own, her eyes sneaked off to look at William only to discover he was looking back at her, his left eyebrow raised, and his lips curved up on that side.

Oh dear. He knew exactly what she'd been doing. She pretended to cough to hide her turmoil.

William became concerned. "You're not ill, are you?"

He pulled Charger closer and patted Louisa on the back. To help with the cough, Louisa was sure, but instead his touch only increased the feeling that she had lost her mooring and drifted toward the unknown.

"I am fine, thank you." She tried to pull Bess away from Charger, but the mare stayed close while William attempted to aid her. "I think I breathed in a little dust."

"You need some water." William saw a stream by the side of the road and jumped from Charger, taking a cup and rag with him.

When he'd moved out of earshot, Louisa took in a deep breath and closed her eyes, forcing herself to imagine cuddly little animals and birds, and even her darling nephews and nieces cavorting in sunlit meadows, until her thoughts were under control.

"Here you are." He handed the cup to her.

She allowed a few drops of the cool liquid to dribble down her throat. "Thank you." She closed her eyes again and relaxed, taking a sip of water and slowing her breathing.

Then William began to wipe her face with the cool rag. Her heart began to beat frantically.

He was much like an illness, a creeping weakness of the lungs which also seemed to be affecting her eyes and heart. She thought she would not catch that affliction again. She'd have to be careful not to allow that intense masculinity to sneak up on her. Perhaps if she took him in small doses she could survive their adventure healthy and whole. With the hope she could endure the next few days without becoming completely overset by the temptation William offered, she opened her eyes and was undone by the tenderness she saw in his face.

"Are you all right, Louisa?"

"I am fine," she whispered.

"You are exhausted. I should have realized that you are not used to such a life."

Louisa took the rag to cool the back of her neck.

"I am fine, truly." She took the pretend baby from William's saddle and began to fan herself with it, but the blanket just flopped and provided no breeze. "I'm only a little warm."

"We'll stop early for the night so you can rest."

The thought of spending the night again, in the dark, in such proximity to William with only a goat as chaperone almost threatened to start her coughing again. Instead, she forced a smile and said, "Then we should probably start riding now."

Later, when the goat sat down in the middle of the road and refused to walk any further, William picked up the small animal and draped her over the saddle in front of him.

"Getting milk for babies when you're traveling is certainly a bother," Louisa reflected.

William nodded.

"It would be nice if they made little containers of milk that don't spoil and are handy to carry."

"They do."

"Oh? I haven't seen them. What are they called?"

"Breasts."

"What?" Louisa straightened in the saddle.

"The mother's breasts." A wicked smile filled his eyes and hovered on his lips.

He watched as she closed her eyes and bit her lip, but a chuckle still escaped. "You are terrible. You did that just to embarrass me, didn't you?" She turned to him, eyes sparkling.

"It is easy to do."

"After these days on the road, I am no longer so straitlaced. You cannot make me blush as easily as you used to!"

"Ahh, I can tell that you are greatly changed."

"Yes, and it is wonderful!" Louisa reached her arms out in front of her, crossing them over her chest, as if she was grasping life and clutching it to her. "You men are so fortunate. You get to live this way, running around the country-side, having exciting adventures without stifling restrictions."

"We don't have all that many opportunities to do that."

"Oh, but you do, even as children. I read stories to my sweet nieces about good little girls who do dull girl things. But when I read to my nephews, we read about swordplay and wars and smuggling and all sorts of exhilarating things. And my nieces do needlework while my nephews race through the woods and duel." She waved an arm in front of her as if she was sword fighting. "I wish I could live that way. You men do whatever you want and have all the fun."

"Not always, Louisa. We do have to behave our- selves on occasions."

"Oh, from time to time perhaps, if you choose to, but you don't have to spend your lives in stifling parlors following ridiculous rules with boring people."

"Don't go back," he suggested.

"I wish it were that easy. Of course, I will have to return to polite society but not yet. There are times I wish I were a man!" She threw her arms out in an appeal to the gods.

"Oh, no," he said in a voice dark with knowledge that made her shiver. "It would be a great loss were you a man."

She looked into his eyes. An expression lurked there. He looked at her for just a second with a longing she could almost feel, but when his eyes immediately became cold, she thought she had imagined that earlier yearning.

"You are too kind," she said fatuously and fell back into the polite chatter of society.

"I smell like goat," William said after they found a clearing where they would spend the night. He unsaddled and rubbed the horses down with the blanket from the log baby. "I'll swim and clean up. When do you wish to eat?" He gestured toward the redolent stew he had bought at a farmhouse earlier.

"Let's eat now, while it's still warm." Louisa ladled the thick meal into bowls provided by the farmwife and placed a crusty piece of bread on top while William tied the goat to a tree to graze. "Then I believe I'd like to wash too. Let me know when you are finished." She glanced at his lifted eyebrow. "No, we shall *not* do that together. You are mean to plague me. I shall bathe either before or after you."

When they had finished eating and William had taken himself off to swim, Louisa placed their blankets on flat ground far from each other. Remembering the first night they had spent on the road and her fear the next morning at hearing someone outside, she searched the forest for a sturdy branch. She found one, longer than her arm and solid, but it was too heavy to pick up, which would not help her in a dangerous situation.

Unable to find a suitable weapon, she placed the wooden baby by her blanket to use as a club. She folded her shawl to use as a pillow, then sat and tried to ignore the fact that William was bathing in the stream, close enough for her to hear the splashing water. A few minutes of silence followed before she heard him come through the bushes.

"I'm finished." He walked into the clearing as light had begun to fade. His hair was wet and clung to his head, curling around his forehead while drips fell on broad, bare shoulders.

"I washed my shirt." He hung it up on a tree.

His torso was bare. His broad chest was bare. Louisa wished she could stop repeating the words broad and bare but her mind had clutched them and refused to let them go.

"Oh my!"

"What did you say?"

"Oh my, you look fresh and clean. I think I'll wash now." She leaped to her feet and staggered on wobbly legs but held her hand up as William started toward her. "No, I am fine, just jealous that you look so fresh and clean."

What had happened to her vocabulary? She sounded like a laundry maid. "You just dry off. I shall be back shortly."

Louisa stumbled into the shadows of the trees and turned away from the clearing, thinking of the cool water and nice bath that lay ahead. Feeling the goat butting her gently, she patted the little animal's head before she took off her dress, placed it over a bush and walked to the stream. There was a larger rock on the edge that would keep her dry but allow her to reach the water. Louisa took off her boots and tattered under-clothes before she untied the unmentionables, allowing them to fall around her ankle, and stepped out of them. After she lowered herself onto the rock, Louisa put her feet into the water and sighed as its coolness flooded through her. She wadded the chemise up and used the undergarment as a cloth to bathe herself, attempting to scrub off the worst of the dirt.

After that, she put her head underwater and rubbed her hair, then lifted it and allowed the water to trickle down her neck and shoulders, reveling in the feel of the breeze against her wet body. The slight wind brought the scent of pine trees. Louisa looked up into the darkening sky at the stars on the horizon. What a marvelous evening. Finally, she filled her hands with water and rinsed her face. It felt refreshing against skin made tender by the sun and wind.

When she finished, she got out of the water and carefully ran her fingers over her legs with her fingers but could feel only a few scabs. She wished she could wash out the unmentionables but didn't know how long it would take for them to dry. She needed to wear them to ride in the morning.

Finally she squeezed the chemise out, picked up her boots, and stood. After pulling on her unmentionables and slipping wet feet into her boots, she hung the chemise on a branch before returning to where she'd spread her dress. It wasn't there.

"William, do you have my dress?"

"Who? Me?"

"Yes, you. Who else is in this clearing?"

"Why would I want it?" When Louisa did not answer, William said, "I assure you I do not!"

"Well, then where—?" The goat butted Louisa's thigh again. Trailing behind the animal was her dress. Louisa grabbed it and held it up. "Your goat has eaten my dress!"

"Let me see." He started into the forest.

"No! You stay where you are! I'll tell you about it." Louisa studied the garment. Fortunately, the animal had only torn off a sleeve and eaten part of the back. Louisa put the dress on. The front was unharmed and she could tie the back shut but her left sleeve was gone and she could feel the breeze against her back. She hung her chemise higher than the goat could reach and returned to the clearing holding her arms across her chest. "At least I can still wear it."

"It looks all right, except, of course, for the sleeve." William stood. "Did she eat any more? Let me see."

Louisa backed against a tree. "No, thank you. I appreciate your concern but there is a great deal of *me* showing. Would you hand me my shawl?"

When he did, she draped it over her shoulder and back. "I feel refreshed from the bath but am so angry at your stupid goat. It is not as if I had an entire wardrobe to choose from."

"Don't shout at me or complain about the poor little animal! She thought you left her a treat." William smiled.

"I can most certainly shout at you! *You* brought that fiendish, dress-eating creature here."

"Now, now, you can't blame me. How did I know you'd leave your dress where she could feast upon it?"

Louisa didn't answer but lay down with her back to William, wrapped herself in the blanket and closed her eyes.

But she could hear him. He attempted to stifle his laughter, but finally he broke into whoops and couldn't stop. She put the blanket over her head but could still hear him.

"I'm sorry, Louisa. It must be terrible for you."

But she knew he didn't really mean it. His voice

quivered and, when he finished the apology, he broke into laughter again.

Louisa slowly woke up, aware of a rustling in the bushes. She opened her eyes. It was dark. There were only a few stars and the moon hid behind a cloud. She held still when the noise came again. There was someone close to them, moving quietly but making enough noise to have awakened her. She had no weapon except the pretend baby and no way to let William know that they were not alone. Of course, he probably already knew.

As silently as possible, she grasped the baby and stood, moving slowly and as quietly as she could toward the trees. She stood completely still when two men entered the clearing.

"I would stop were I you," William said from the other side of the open space. "I have pistols and can shoot both of you."

"Ahh," came a voice from behind Louisa, "but I have the lady and will shoot her if you hurt my friends."

For a moment, she held herself motionless and silent to ascertain exactly where the man behind her stood. "Don't listen to him!" she shouted. "Kill those two and save the baby."

The man reached down, touched the soft blanket and shouted, "And I have the baby too."

With that, Louisa swung the fake baby around and hit the man on the side of the head with a satisfying clunk. He fell.

"I got him," she yelled. Then she tore the blanket from the log baby and hit the man again.

Frightened by the ruckus, the goat began to bleat softly from where she was hobbled. When he heard the noise, one of the men shouted, "The baby!" They both ran toward the sound as Louisa dropped the log and dashed across the clearing toward William.

The man she had hit had begun to wake up. "She hit me with the baby!" he shouted.

"This will give us a little time," William said as he tossed Louisa on Bess and he jumped on Charger.

"Shut up," they heard another man say. "She wouldn't hit you with the baby."

William grabbed his shirt from the tree as they rode by it. "Can you ride without a saddle?"

"I love it." Louisa pointed to the left. "Their horses are tied over there."

As the men scrambled through the brush after them, William loosened the reins of their mounts. Spooked by the commotion, the three horses took off as two of the men broke through the bushes, but one of the spies whistled and his horse slowed.

Charger and Bess took off quickly with William and Louisa leaning low in case the men started shooting at them.

"We're going to have to ride hard. Are you up to it?" William called over his shoulder to Louisa.

"Lead on!" She laughed as the wind blew her hair out behind her.

Chapter Nine

"**A**re we still in danger?" Louisa asked after hours of hard riding, during which her legs reminded her they had not yet completely healed. The sun had risen an hour previously, and the songs of birds had quieted from trees towering thick and tall on both sides of the road.

"I believe so," William said. From the start of their flight, he'd chosen lanes that led in different directions, going south then west before they rode east. They stopped for an afternoon meal at a small inn where he'd bought saddles for each of them, then rode on until the sun had set.

"I remember a small and fairly secluded inn ahead where we can stop," William said hours later. "Tired?"

She sat up and smiled. "No, I'm ready to ride all

night." In truth, she was exhausted, and thought her legs had frozen into permanent curves like the bowed legs on her aunt's Egyptian chaise but she would have died before telling him that. Of course, he knew, from interpreting her drooping body but she'd still not admit it. "Do we have to?"

"No, we can rest."

The horses stepped faster as they entered the small stable where William ordered an extra portion of oats for them. In the private parlor, Louisa stuffed every bite of dinner in her mouth, wiped up the gravy with a piece of warm bread, and washed it down with a delicious ale. Although not quite up to the standards of Arnold's chef, the food tasted better than anything she could remember eating.

After dinner, she leaned back to enjoy the soft cushion on the chair and the comfort of this cozy room filled with the smoke of the fire and the lingering smells of dinner. She took another sip of ale and felt its warmth slide down her throat. Shortly, she'd be able to wash up and sleep in a bed.

Louisa glanced at William. How very handsome he looked. In her relaxed and drowsy state, she allowed herself to study him from beneath her heavy eyelids. His lips were drawn straight and tight, and his eyes refused to meet hers. Her drowsy reverie was broken by the nervous way his fingers drummed on the table.

"What's the matter?" she asked. "Are we still in danger?"

"It's not only that." He paused before he took a deep breath and said in a rush. "We have to share a room."

"We are sharing a room?" She sat straight. "The inn didn't look that crowded."

"No, that's not the reason." He glanced away then his eyes met hers before again becoming unreadable. "I have to make sure you are safe. I can't do that if we're not in the same room."

"Of course not." The idea of being in the same bed-chamber with William would make her feel safe but it really wasn't proper. Not a bit. But after spending a few nights in the woods with him, propriety hardly mattered.

A little lightheaded from exhaustion and the excellent ale, as if in a dream, she stretched her hand out and traced his arched eyebrow with her index finger then followed that line down his cheek and across his neck. Their eyes met and held, then he took her hand as he leaned forward and tilted his head.

He's going to kiss me. Her lips moved towards him as his breath blew gently against her cheek. His mouth was close enough to hers that she could feel its warmth.

Instead, he sat back. "We are going to have to marry, you realize. We cannot share a room without being married."

"William, I will not marry you just because circumstance has thrown us into this situation."

"We must, Louisa, whether we want to or not."

She studied him. "I would prefer a better reason, William."

"Ahh, I know you want to marry for love. You need to learn to be more realistic."

She nodded. "Perhaps I don't want to be realistic, at least not in the way society thinks about marriage." Enjoying the comfort of the room and the warmth of the ale, she paused before continuing. "When I was young, my mother was very ill. One night I was so worried that I got out of bed and went into her room. My father sat next to her bed, holding her hand. He was crying." She stopped and thought about that moment. "He said to her, 'Please get well. Do not leave me, for you are my heart, and I cannot live without you.'"

"That's a nice story, Louisa, but hardly the way most marriages are."

"That's why I haven't married. I want to marry a man who cannot live without me." She smiled up at him. "If you cannot offer me that, I will not marry you."

He stared at her and started to speak, only to be interrupted when the door opened. "My lord, I have prepared your room," the innkeeper said.

"Thank you. If you will take my wife up, I will follow shortly."

Louisa turned back toward him when she heard herself being called his wife but, of course, why else would they be sharing a room but as a married couple?

"Don't be long." She stood and turned back to him.

He had almost, for a moment, wished he could be the man who could fulfill her dreams. Only for a moment though did he want to say those words as if he meant them. Perhaps he did. After all, she was brave and lovely, and being married to her wouldn't be as bad as marriage with some. He could have said those words when they were young.

What an idiot he'd become over the years, a cynic. And, he realized with a shrug, a man of honor. As he contemplated the fire, he realized he continued to put Louisa in terrible danger for no reason. He didn't need her to care for the baby and they had drawn the enemy away from the child. For her sake, he'd leave her here, ride away, and lead the spies away from her.

He'd leave Charger for her. His steed could run for hours. No one would be able to catch her before she could arrive at the estate of one of her siblings. Yes, he would leave her in safety, but not tonight. They had ridden for hours, and he was exhausted. He needed sleep. He'd leave early in the morning.

He called the innkeep and asked for a paper and pen. Although the pen splattered ink, he finally completed a farewell letter which he folded and hid in the waist of his trousers. He called for a pitcher of warm water and carried it upstairs.

When he entered, she was in bed. Her clothes were hung on hooks, and the basin was still damp from her ablutions.

"Thank you for having the innkeeper get a night-gown from his wife for me." When she smiled at him, his heart held still. "She is evidently a large woman."

"You're welcome." He put the pitcher down, then turned toward the torn blue gown and held it up. "I didn't realize how much the goat ate. We'll see if the innkeep's wife has one I can buy for you."

He poured warm water in the basin and washed his face. When he pulled his shirt off to wash his body, he glanced over his shoulder at her. She was decorously facing the wall.

"I'm finished," he told her after he'd put the shirt back on. He began to arrange the chair and a stool to sleep on.

"What are you doing?"

"Making a place to sleep."

Louisa turned, keeping careful hold on the overlarge gown. "There's plenty of room on the bed. Don't you want to sleep on the other side?"

"My dear, do you not know that were you and I to share the bed, we'd not rest tonight?" A blush spread across her face, visible even in the small amount of light. "Now, go to sleep. I'll see you in the morning," he lied.

Filling his memory with her, he watched her as she pulled the covers around her and fell asleep. When he was sure his movements wouldn't awaken her, he took out the note and placed it on the dresser next to her clothes. Then he settled himself in the chair and told himself to wake up in five hours.

He could hear her soft breathing and wished he could share the bed with her then watch her awaken in the morning. Instead, he watched Louisa sleep until weariness overtook him.

When he awakened, the sun had begun to rise. He stood and walked silently to the bed to look down at Louisa. Her lovely hair spread around her on the pillow. He picked up a strand and curled it around his finger. Although he knew it might awaken her, he wanted to kiss her—just once, in case he never saw her again, but he didn't dare chance waking her. He told himself what he felt was desire, not love, and maybe it was the memory of what they'd shared as youngsters, but he couldn't quite make himself believe it. He studied her for a heartbeat then loosened the curl, turned and silently left the room.

An hour later, Louisa woke up to noise in the stable yard outside her window. "William," she murmured, "what's that?" When he didn't answer, she rolled over and looked at the chair. He wasn't there. Anxious, she looked around the empty room. She was alone. With a leap, she was out of bed and at the window in two steps. Below, three men on horses shouted at the stableboy. He listened, then pointed to the north and said something. One man nodded and threw him a coin as they rode off.

Louisa grabbed her clothes and began to dress. She'd finished pulling on the unmentionables and thrown the ripped dress on before she saw the note. Slowly and with a sense of deep dread, she picked the paper up and read:

I've gone ahead on Bess to draw them away from you. Take Charger and ride as fast as you can to the home of one of your brothers or sisters and stay there. Stay there!

It was signed with a scrawled W.

"You stupid, stupid man!" she shouted and threw the note on the floor. After pulling on her boots and grabbing her shawl, she picked up the handkerchief with the coins in it and ran downstairs, her hair streaming behind her.

"Your husband has paid the bill," the innkeeper said. "He wanted to make sure you got a good rest so he rode ahead to take care of business, he said. I hope you feel better."

"Yes, I'm much better, thank you." She tied the coins in the corner of her shawl and raced outside, toward the stable.

"How could you do it?" she shouted at the stableboy. "How could you tell those men where my . . . my husband went?"

"Pardon, missus?"

She stopped her shouting and said, "I saw you. You told those three men where my husband was."

"Your husband told me to. He paid me to tell 'em the wrong direction."

"What?"

"He went that way"—the boy pointed east—"but he told me to tell them he went that way." He pointed north.

"When did he leave?"

"Oh, a little after dawn."

"Get my horse ready."

He went in the barn and returned in a few minutes with Charger. "Your husband wanted to buy you a lady's saddle, but it wasn't big enough for this fellow. It would have fit your little mare just fine, but your husband wanted you to have his horse so you could ride fast to your sister's home."

She stepped in the hands the stableboy held for her and threw herself across the horse. "He wanted me to ride fast, and I'm going to do that. He rode that way?" She pointed east. "Did he mention where he was going?"

"No, ma'am. Said to tell you not to go north or east, that you should go to your sister's where they was waiting for you."

"Thank you." Louisa tied her shawl firmly around her neck and rode off with the shouts of the stableboy fading away behind her.

He yelled, "No, missus, he said for you *not* to go east!"

But she did. She rode east, after that hardheaded,

heroic fool who had forgotten they were a team and were not to be split up just because he wanted to protect her. Didn't he know she didn't want to be safe if it meant being away from him?

She kicked Charger and shouted for the steed to go at top speed, trusting that somehow she'd find him as they rode east into the sun.

Louisa guessed he'd follow the main highway and that he wouldn't travel too fast in an attempt to lead the men away from her, in case they paid the stableboy more than he had. She pushed Charger along the road and searched as the landscape streamed by the galloping horse. They went through several villages where people stared at the strange sight of a woman astride the large mount and moving like a fury with her hair blowing behind her.

She passed farmland and over bridges, through wooded areas, and paused at streams to allow Charger to drink. The heavy animal rode steadily and easily, not needing to slow or rest.

It was three hours after he left the inn when he saw her. She had almost ridden by without seeing him, and he'd hoped she would. He stood in a field while Bess grazed, and had looked off in the distance when the fast movements of a horse and rider caught his attention. He recognized Charger almost immediately and knew that the rider was angry.

Like a coward, he tried to pull Bess into a grove of trees in the hope they could hide before Louisa could find them, but he knew the moment her eyes found him. She pulled Charger to a halt and sat up in the stirrups, glaring at him. He pulled Bess more quickly toward the grove.

"Fool," he called himself. It was pointless to hide from her in the trees because she'd certainly follow, but he still sought momentary refuge. He wished he could vanish. Before he could completely disappear, Charger galloped up to him and Louisa threw herself off the horse, landed on him, and began to beat him with her fists.

"Why did you leave me? How could you leave me again?" she shouted.

"What are you doing here, Louisa? Can't you do anything right?" He took her hands and held them down to her side while he berated her. "You are the most stubborn woman. Why didn't you do what I told you to?"

"How could you leave me?" she demanded in a soft voice.

"I wanted you safe. Wasn't that obvious?"

"I thought we worked together."

"I wanted you to be safe."

"I wanted to be with you." She looked up at him, her eyes like velvet pansies sprinkled with dew. "I wanted to be with you," she whispered.

"And I wanted you to be out of danger."

"I don't want to be out of danger." She pulled her arms from his grasp and flung them around his neck, pressing against him. "I want to be with you," she whispered and pulled his lips to hers.

He'd had to teach her to kiss when she was seventeen. She hadn't forgotten a thing. Then Louisa's fingers crept into his hair and began to rub marvelous patterns into his scalp and down his neck.

After a pleasurable moment, sanity forced its way into his brain. It took every bit of willpower but he pushed her away from him and draped the shawl over her shoulders. "Louisa, not now," he said in his most reasonable voice. "We need to head for safety."

"For now." She took a step toward him. "I'd like a kiss. Just one more kiss."

"No, Louisa, this is not that time." He pointed toward the horses. "Now, get on Bess." When she didn't move, he added in his sternest, most threatening voice, "Immediately."

Relief filled him when she pulled Bess to a log and mounted her because he had no idea what he would have done if she hadn't. He took Charger's reins and mounted also.

"I want you to take Bess and ride as fast as she'll go to the estate of one of your relatives and stay there," he ordered. "As many brothers and sisters as you have, we must be close to the estate of one of them. I want you to get yourself to a place of safety, and I'll carry on alone."

"I know what you want, but I'm not going to do it." She glared at him haughtily. "Not by myself."

"Lord save me from bossy women!" William hit his forehead with the palm of his hand.

"You don't have to worry about bossy women. Would you just listen to me?" She sat with her arms crossed and glared at him.

"Louisa, you have me confused with one of your nephews. You can't intimidate me with that formidable look. It is time for you to return to your home and your family."

"William, I know that. I know where we are," she explained slowly. "There's no need for you to keep going or for me either! We're very close to Cosden Park, the estate of my sister Julianna's husband."

"Then you go there, and I will keep riding."

"Can't you stop being the hero for a moment? We can go to Cosden Park together. Certainly we've done our part. We've led the spies far afield. They have no idea where to find little Bea, and the Durwoods will keep her safe. If we disappear now, won't that confuse them, William? I do love the adventure, but perhaps we could get a bath and sleep in beds and get clean clothes before we continue, if we need to continue."

William looked off in the distance. "Warm bath, huh?" He didn't speak for another minute. "Very well, Louisa. I've considered everything and must admit that the idea of a bath and clean clothes has won me over. Lead the way."

Chapter Ten

When Louisa and William approached Cosden Park, it was obvious they had landed themselves in a bumblebroth. There were carriages in the drive. Women in pastels and looking like spring flowers promenaded through the great sweep of lawn at the front of the mansion, while gentlemen in dark coats watched from benches scattered under trees and on the broad terrace.

Cosden Park was one of the largest and most elegant estates in the country. A beautiful columned Palladian entrance stood out against a building covered with pillars, cornices, pergolas, and loggias, all of which gave the building an oddly lopsided, asymmetrical but imposing appearance.

"We cannot go to the front door like this." Louisa surveyed their disreputable condition. "Cosden is somewhat high in the instep."

"You're too kind. I would call him a snob, but not even the most gracious of hosts would welcome us as we are now." William looked down at himself. "We cannot go in the servants' entrance either. They would toss us out."

"Perhaps if we were to wash up. There's a pond around the side of the house."

They looked at each other and laughed. William's shirt was ragged and filthy; his face was covered with several days of dark whiskers; and his unmentionables were a greasy brown.

Louisa knew she looked even worse. The shawl didn't completely cover the gaping hole in the back of her dress, and her arm showed bare from the elbow down. Grimy unmentionables showed beneath the faded blue skirt of Mrs. Durwood's dress. The only barely presentable articles on either of them were their boots although his had long since lost their champagne shine and hers were covered with scratches and dust. Not even a long bath in the pond would make them presentable.

"No, the servants wouldn't allow us in nor would any of the tenants." Louisa grimaced. "I'll have to smuggle a note to Julianna."

"How will you do that? We have nothing to write

with and nothing to write on. I hope you don't think I'm going to go to the door through that crowd! From here I recognize Godwell and Fothergill and a host of others."

"*I* certainly can't go. I would be ruined were I recognized."

"Then we'll stay here." He climbed off Charger, tied him to a bush and sat down in the shade.

"But you're a spy! Are you not trained for this by the government? Do you not have any ideas of what we should do in such a situation?" She leaped from Bess and stood in front of him.

"If I were a spy, and I am not, I would not be in such a situation. I suggest we wait until dark and break a window."

"Oh, that's foolish. Darkness is hours away." She stamped her foot. "I'm hungry and dirty."

"Then what would you have us do?"

"I'm going to sneak in some way."

"How will you do that?"

"Everyone is in the front so we should be able to get in the back fairly well. Come with me." She took his hand and tugged until he was forced to stand. "If we leave the horses here and go around this side of the house, there are bushes to screen us from the guests."

"Unless, of course, they too are wandering around this side of the house."

"Oh, no, Cosden would never allow that. He expects his guests to stay where he puts them."

"Ahh, yes, Cosden always was an autocrat. Must be

keeping with his title. Dukes, after all, are above us mortals. He sounds as imperious as his sister by marriage."

"Shh!" Louisa grabbed his hand and pulled him behind ornaments shrubs. They sneaked around the side of the immense building.

It happened, Louisa was sure as she lay on the ground, because she'd been laughing at some absurdity William whispered and forgotten about the ha-ha. Whatever the reason, she fell in before she remembered the location of the sunken fence, and William tumbled in the hole behind her. In fact, right on top of her. As he twisted his body to lay next to her, she turned over to face him. "Are you all right?"

"Oh, I had a delightfully soft landing." He rubbed his hand across her cheek. "But you fell on the ground and then had me land right on top of you. Are you hurt?"

He peered down at her with the expression he'd had before he kissed her before. She wished he would. In the hope of such an outcome, Louisa placed her left arm around his neck. With her right hand, she rubbed his cheek and guided his lips toward hers. "You will need to shave before you meet polite company."

"Ahh, yes. However, I am pleased the shameless little baggage beneath me seems to appreciate whiskers." He lowered his head to kiss her when a voice thundered above them.

"Dutton, Dutton, come here! There are two scoundrels making love in my ha-ha."

Oh, drat! Louisa opened her eyes and saw, as she had expected, her brother-in-law standing over them. "Hello, Cosden."

His eyes almost flew from their sockets when he heard the dirty creature use his name. Cosden patted his lip with a lace-embroidered handkerchief and demanded, "Who are you? How dare you talk to me?"

"It is I, Louisa. Julianna's sister."

"Oh my goodness." He patted his round face with the cloth. "What in heaven's name are you doing in my ha-ha? Who is the degenerate handling you?"

William stood slowly and reluctantly. "Hello, Cosden. The degenerate is Woodstone."

"Woodstone? What in the name of God are you doing dressed like that, cuddling with my wife's sister in my ha-ha?" The duke stood with his mouth opening and closing and emitted little gagging sounds while his hands fluttered.

Reaching out to help Louisa to her feet, William said, "Perhaps it would be better for us to discuss this inside."

"Inside?" The duke's voice shot up an octave. "But you are so terribly and completely and disgustingly *dirty*. Absolutely filthy. You cannot wish to enter Cosden Park in that condition."

Louisa allowed William to boost her out of the ha-ha before he climbed out himself. "Where would you like to discuss this further, Cosden?" she asked. "We could go to the front terrace."

"Oh, no, no." Cosden sniffed. "Whatever is that

stench?" He waved his handkerchief at them then, real-
izing the odor came from the two of them, placed the
square over his nose.

"Well, we certainly cannot clean up out here,"
Louisa pointed out. "Earlier I suggested a bath in your
pond but William thought not. Sometimes he is too nice
in his opinions."

"Now be fair," William objected. "You decided it
would do no good but perhaps we should reconsider if
Cosden will not extend his hospitality to us."

"Louisa, I do not understand what has happened to
you," Cosden murmured, his words slightly muffled by
the handkerchief. "You used to be the most compatible
of your sister's family, as nice in your actions and opinions as I could ever have hoped. Now I find you dirty
and disporting yourself in my ha-ha with this reprobate.
My dear, it does not bear discussion."

"Reprobate?" Louisa looked at William questioningly.

"Are you going to leave us out here? Perhaps we
should go to the parkland and join your guests,"
William said.

"No, no! The gossip! It is not to be considered. Why
don't you go into the greenhouse." He waved his handkerchief toward a wing on the end of the rambling pile
of a house.

"Dutton!" He motioned to the man in the livery who
approached. "Please find her grace and bring her to the
greenhouse."

When Dutton glanced at Louisa and William, his

nose ascended, but he said not a word before he turned to carry out the duke's orders.

"I do not believe there is anything you can sully or spoil in the greenhouse." Cosden explained. "There are some wooden benches which can be burned after you leave. The fruit there should cover the stench. Best of all," he stated with a sigh of relief, "none of our guests can see you there."

Only moments after they entered the greenhouse, Julianna hurried in from the door which led to the mansion. "Louisa." She threw out her arms to embrace her sister before the odor hit her. "Oh, my!" She dropped her arms and leaped away from the smell and dirt, then scurried to stand next to her husband at a prudent distance, the skirt of her lovely rose gown lifted to keep it from contamination.

As Julianna scrutinized her sister, she lifted one eyebrow and pursed pink lips. "Whatever have you been doing? Wherever have you been?"

"When I found her," Cosden said as he moved behind a row of orange trees and removed the handkerchief from his nose, "she and Woodstone were in the ha-ha, cuddling."

"Oh," Julianna gasped. She blinked. "Louisa was cuddling with Woodstone in the ha-ha?"

"We didn't mean to cuddle," Louisa said. "We fell in, and William was on top of me."

Julianna fell against her husband with a shriek.

"I will explain." William guided Louisa to a bench

where they both sat. "But later. Right now, we are dirty and tired and hungry."

"Oh yes." Julianna went to the door and asked Dutton to have a luncheon tray brought.

"Let me tell you what happened." Turning toward Louisa, William said, "Cosden, as you're aware from earlier discussions we've had in Whitehall, we have an invaluable spy . . ."

The tea tray came during the middle of William's story of their escape with the baby. He and Louisa devoured every piece of bread and cake as well as some delightful lemon tarts and other delicacies they could not identify in their haste. Finally, they emptied the teapot while Julianna and Cosden watched in fascination.

After William finished the story between bites, Cosden looked at him, then turned to his wife. "My dear, why don't you take your sister inside and help her clean up. Woodstone and I will make some arrangements."

After the two women left, Cosden turned toward William. "You will, of course, marry her."

"I have proposed and been turned down. Twice."

"Why would she do that?" The duke continued to observe William from a safe distance.

"Something about love."

"Ahh, yes. Women are like that. My duchess had the same foolish idea until I convinced her marriage has nothing to do with emotion."

"I am sure she got over that folly very quickly after marrying you."

"Of course." Cosden nodded imperiously. "Have no fear. My duchess will speak to Louisa about her duty and explain what she must do for her family. Of course, knowing Louisa . . . although she is a most refined woman." He sighed.

"However, there are times she is not the most *manageable* of women," William observed.

"No, not at all submissive at times." He fixed William with a withering glare. "Nonetheless, Woodstone, I shall expect you to ask her again and to convince her to take such a step. You are, after all, a gentleman, I have heard, with a great deal of address." He frowned. "You must persuade her to marry you. It is your duty to protect her from scandal and she must accept to shield her family from dishonor."

"Ahh, yes, I should appeal to her guilt and shame."

"It usually works with women." Cosden's speech became very slow and clear. "I am certain you do understand your duty."

William had never liked Cosden. *Conceited* did not begin to describe him. Snob, prude . . . he could think of many other words to describe him.

No, although William trusted and respected the duke, he could not like him. For Cosden to lecture him as if he was a scruffy little boy, well, it rankled.

Finally Cosden stood. "It is still early in the day. I'm going to have Dutton take you to an inn close by while a footman takes a message to your man. He is in London?" At William's nod, he continued. "Good, that is a distance of only two hours. I will send a message to him immediately. He will need to bring you clothing and your vehicle so that you will be dressed to come to the house party tonight. I will expect you by seven-thirty, before dinner, to speak with Louisa."

Cosden held his quizzing glass to his eye and fixed William with his resolute glare. "You will ask her to marry you. Again. And this time you *will* convince her to do so."

"Yes, Cosden, but wouldn't it be easier for my man to come here to Cosden Park immediately? Why should I stay at the inn?"

"Easier, perhaps, for you, but ruinous to Louisa should our guests discover the two of you arrived at the same time. Only imagine what people might believe! Oh my!" He put his hand on his chest and sighed in dismay. "My duchess and I will think of a tale of why Louisa happens to be here. You must come tonight very publicly so no one could possibly connect your entrance with hers."

"Then I shall go to London—"

"No." Cosden spoke like a king to a commoner. "You will go to the inn with Dutton so he can shave and bathe you while you await your clothing and coach. Once you are presentable, you will come here and beg Lady Louisa to accept you in marriage. Have I made myself clear?"

William nodded. Cosden had made it very clear what he had to do.

* * *

"Oh, dearest!" Julianna walked to her chamber at a distance from Louisa. "You must have had a terrible time! You look dreadful." An odd look passed over her face. "And the odor. What is it?"

"Goat, I believe. If not that, perhaps there was something else in the hay."

Upon entering her bedroom, Julianna called for a maid whom she sent with instructions for a bath to be brought immediately. "And, while you are bathing, I shall write a note to Boswell—is she at Longtrees? She should be able to arrive by tomorrow. You can wear my gowns and share my dresser until then.

"Now, please do not sit down or touch anything!" Julianna begged her sister, then spread a sheet on the floor. "There, stand in the middle of that and take off those horrible clothes." She shuddered. "Wrap yourself in this." She pulled another cover from the bed and tossed it to Louisa. "We shall talk while you bathe." Julianna paused. "You know you must marry Woodstone."

"We shall talk about that when I am clean and comfortable," Louisa replied in a voice every bit as resolute as her sister's.

The water, warm and scented with lilac, felt wonderful. Louisa rubbed the soap into her hair and worked it into a lather before rinsing it and allowing the water to run down her body, to clean away days of filth. She laughed upon seeing hay floating on the surface of the bath.

"I see nothing amusing about your situation," Julianna said.

"No, you wouldn't. But the old Julianna, the Julianna of ten years ago, she would have joined the adventure with me."

"I am not, I am glad to say, the heedless Julianna of my childhood. I am a duchess and, as such, I have a position of prominence to guard."

"Yes, dear sister, I know, but I am not a duchess, and I had such a wonderful time."

Julianna pulled a wooden chair close to the tub. "And are you still a . . . um . . . unblemished?"

"Of course I am. Woodstone was a perfect gentleman."

Julianna fell against the back of the chair. "That is hard to believe of him. Still, as a gentleman, he must marry you. Cosden will make sure he comes up to scratch."

"He asked me to marry him. Twice. I refused, both times."

Julianna struggled with her breathing. "You refused him? Twice? Oh, Louisa, how could you?"

"I do not wish to marry a man who is forced to marry me. Who would?"

"Well, of course not, but I'm sure he will see his duty and will *want* to marry you."

"I do not wish to marry a man who feels marriage to me is his duty."

"What do you know about Woodstone?" Julianna asked thoughtfully.

"Oh, I admit, not much. I knew him when we were much younger. I know he is devoted to his country." Louisa slid further into the warm water.

"Which is of great importance in a marriage, of course."

"Oh, Julianna, I know it isn't. You have lost every bit of your sense of humor."

"Louisa, this is not the time for jesting."

"Yes, Julianna, but you did ask what I knew about him." She closed her eyes and enjoyed the feel of the water. "I haven't seen him in years, and he was a nice young man back then."

"Have you met him recently? During the season?"

"No, it seems that we have missed each other. When I was in London, he was not. When he was, I was not."

"Even if you spent the same seasons in London, you probably would not have seen him. He never attended Almack's nor did he frequent any of the fêtes of the marriage mart. He is more likely in a gambling hell."

Louisa said nothing in reply. She knew her sister would continue without prompting.

"He has been seen with many women but never seemed interested in marriage."

"He said he wasn't." Louisa sat up to reach for a towel, her movement causing the water to overflow and splash her sister's lovely morning dress.

"Oh, Louisa! How could you make even more of a mess?" Julianna leaped to her feet, grabbed a towel, and attempted to soak the water from her skirt.

"I am sorry, Julianna, but you have a closet full of beautiful gowns." She took the towel, stood, and stepped from the tub to dry herself.

"Louisa, you and I must discuss this rapscallion with whom you have spent the last few days completely unchaperoned."

"Oh, not completely. Titania was there for a day or two, and I spent one night on the floor of the Durwoods' cottage. And there was the goat." She wrapped a towel around her and picked up another to dry her hair.

"Let us not trivialize or attempt to make light of this, Louisa. You are thoroughly ruined."

"Not if no one finds out what happened." Louisa looked at her sister in the way that usually quieted her but this time it did not work.

"You must marry Woodstone. There is no other alternative. He must offer for you, and you *must* accept him."

"I do not want to marry him if he does not want to marry me. I cannot imagine a worse way to spend the rest of my life."

"You still expect to love the man you marry?"

"Irrational, am I not?" Louisa smiled which obviously infuriated Julianna.

"Yes you are, and foolish. The world does not function like that. There are husbands and wives who love each other, but that is not the usual way of things. Cosden and I are perfectly happy together without any unseemly sentiment to destroy the tranquility of our union."

"I know you are. Darling, if you are content to live like that, I would not expect you to behave in any other way." Louisa put on a nightgown Julianna had laid out for her and began to brush her damp hair. "But I could not exist that way. If I am ruined, then I will find a nice little house and live with my horse and get a dog or perhaps a goat. I can afford that and much more. I would be happier there than living in a marriage without love."

"Oh, Louisa!"

"Yes, I know. You despair of me. I'm sorry to be such a problem." She stifled a yawn.

As Julianna continued to chatter, trying to bring her sister to her senses, Louisa fell asleep and dreamed of a dark man driving a wagon along the back roads in Essex and cuddling with her in the ha-ha.

"You look lovely. Don't fuss." Julianna inspected her dresser's efforts with Louisa.

Louisa had moved to another bedroom once she had rested. After an afternoon spent chatting with members of the house party and renewing old acquaintances, she had changed for the ball that evening in a dress Julianna had chosen from her wardrobe.

"This dress displays entirely too much of me for my peace of mind." Louisa protested as she attempted to pull the neckline high. It was a fashionable gown of sky blue with lovely piping around the hem.

"It most certainly does not!" Julianna drew herself up and frowned at her sister. "It is one of my newest and most fashionable dresses, and you may be sure I do not order dresses that are in poor taste. Of course, you have always been a bit of a prude about clothing."

"A what?" Louisa swirled to look at her sister. "Do you think I am . . . prim?"

"Yes dear, you can be, but we all love you."

"Oh. Straitlaced?"

"I would not go that far, although Edward has said . . ."

"You have discussed me with Lucinda and Edward? And he believes I am straitlaced?" Louisa took a lock of her hair that the dresser had carefully placed to curl down her neck, and pushed it back into her braid. "Well, I believe Edward is a prissy bore."

"Well, yes, he is, but let's not discuss our family any further." Julianna tugged the lock from Louisa's braid, curled it around her finger and dropped it so it softened her sister's normal style.

"That looks ridiculous."

"Nonsense. It is fetching." Julianna stood back to look at her sister. "You are really lovely when you are dressed correctly."

"What do you mean *correctly*? I always go to the best modistes and dress in the height of fashion."

"Yes, but the height of fashion for a grandmother. You are enchanting tonight. If you cannot convince that man to marry you when you look so very lovely, I wash my hands of you."

"Then prepare your pitcher and basin for I will not accept an unwilling husband."

"It is your job to make him willing, my dear. That is what a woman does."

"Bah," Louisa countered inelegantly.

William was successfully smuggled out of Cosden Park to the inn. Once in a bedroom of the inn, Dutton ordered towels and a bath. He scrubbed, shampooed, and shaved William then left him with instructions not to leave the room until his valet arrived and William was presentable.

William would have bristled under such instructions had not the thorough cleansing felt so wonderful, and were he not so tired. In addition, he really could not leave the room. Dutton had taken his clothes to dispose of and left him with only Cosden's robe.

After Dutton's departure, William wandered around the room, inspecting the furniture for a few minutes before he looked out the window at the yard of the bustling inn.

Finally he realized he could put the decision off no longer, if, indeed, he had a say in the decision. He had to face what awaited him upon his return to Cosden Park.

It was not Louisa that concerned him. He was very attracted to her. It was strange that he felt that way. He had always been interested in showy blonds but her honesty and courage and, yes, beauty, appealed to him greatly.

"Ha," he laughed mirthlessly. Appeal to him? Of course she did and more. He wanted her in his bed, to make love to her, to wake up to find her sleeping against him, to lose himself in her beautiful hair.

But he didn't want to marry her.

Blast Cosden for forcing the decision.

Of course, as a gentleman, he had no choice. Doing the honorable thing was, after all, what his father would have expected as well, which made him hate it even more.

He'd never pleased his father. The old man had found out about his faux pas of falling in love with Louisa all those years ago. He'd lectured William then, and then sent him off to the peninsula to join the other younger sons in fighting Napoleon. He'd hated every minute of it, but he'd learned to lead men.

After the war, his father sent William to Boston to learn from an uncle. *That* experience William had enjoyed. He'd built up a nice fortune for himself, the only thing he'd ever done to please his father.

Then William returned to England and found he took great pleasure in the life of a gentleman. After years of work, he liked the clubs, the gambling, the women.

Did that sound callow and completely selfish? Yes,

but he didn't want to give up that world. He didn't want to stop seeing his opera dancers and high-flyers. Very simply, he didn't know if he could be faithful to one woman. He had no desire to settle down into the life Louisa would expect, the life she deserved. He'd make her miserable. He cared for her enough not to wish for that.

All in all, he was not the man for her, and Cosden had no right to force either one of them into this.

If only he had enough time to sort this out, to discuss this with Louisa without Cosden forcing him. One should not be expected to foil French spies and consider marriage at the same time.

He couldn't deny he liked being with her. There was a magic at times when they were together, a longing to touch and kiss her, a desire to make her happy. Maybe what he felt was more than lust, but was that enough to base a marriage on? Yes, he did like her but he did *not* want to marry her. Not now.

Oh, he had eight years ago, back when he'd been a romantic fool. Even then, he didn't think much of the convention of marriage but he'd been captivated by Louisa. He had given his heart only that one time, and that had ended with an embarrassing lecture from Louisa's father. After that, he had moved on with his life with little problem and no regrets. Surely that showed the shallowness of his affection and character.

His parents' marriage had been a shouting match between a bully and a harridan, and those of his friends weren't much better. They either battled or never spoke to each other. He greatly preferred his bachelor life. He was happy as he was, seeing as many women as he wanted. When he tired of one, he could move on.

Yes, he was shallow and inconsistent and self-centered. Everything he'd told Louisa was true. He could not be the husband she wanted, not one who would cry by her bedside.

He would explain that to Louisa. Perhaps this evening they could discuss the matter rationally, let her realize that marriage to him was not what she wanted. That decided, he sat down and picked up a newspaper Dutton had left with him.

Minutes later, he heard a knock, hours too early for Ivory, his valet. He opened the door to find two men with a tray covered with an enormous meal. He ate then lay down and slept for hours, waking only when he heard Ivory at the door.

By seven o'clock, he was presentable. His frock coat topped tight-fitting breeches, silk stocking and black pumps. His neckcloth was spotless with a large diamond in its snowy folds. He wasn't handsome, he knew, but there was something about him that attracted women with no effort on his part.

Ivory had driven the phaeton while William's clothing arrived in a traveling vehicle driven by his coachman. To go to Cosden Park, the two servants followed in the coach while William tooled down the road in his phaeton, feeling at home in his clean clothing and familiar vehicle but terrified about the coming interview.

At Cosden Park, a butler opened the door and led William to the billiards room where he was welcomed politely by Cosden and heartily by various friends. Fothergill asked him to play billiards but he turned him down, claiming fatigue.

Cosden then called a footman who took William to the chambers he would use for the duration of his stay. As soon as William arrived in the suite, Cosden entered and escorted him down the family stairway to the small parlor where, he feared, his fate awaited him.

Chapter Eleven

The door slammed shut behind William with the finality of a cell door in a jail. In spite of the mild evening, he felt an immediate chill emanating, he thought, from Louisa. Not even the medallioned ceiling, silk drapes and intricately carved furniture of this luxuriously appointed parlor could make it feel warm and welcoming.

Louisa turned when he entered. With her hair dressed softly and becomingly, she looked so lovely he had to beat down the instant response the sight of her awakened.

She wore a fashionable gown. Of course she did. This one was of a blue that made her hair shimmer, turned her eyes to a deep shade of blue, and brought a glow to her fair skin. It clung to her in a way that made

161

him swallow several times. She had a brilliance, an allure, an air of confidence both the younger Louisa and Miss Prim had lacked.

But as she watched him enter the room, her eyes grew cold. Probably she could tell from the stiffness of his stance and the banked fury in his eyes that he was there only because he had been forced to appear. If she hadn't realized the entire disaster galled him, then he'd lost his ability to communicate his emotions without sharing them.

Why should *she* have her nose out of joint? Why should *she* look as if she didn't wish to see him, as if *she* preferred not to be here? Why did she lift her chin and avert her eyes as if he was lower than one of the insects that had plagued them on their mad ride?

It wasn't as if she'd been lectured by Cosden like a small, dirty underclassman of little importance. And yet, as much as he attempted to ignore it, the voice of fairness said Louisa had probably been scolded by her sister.

Her gaze roamed over his black coat, embroidered waistcoat and light unmentionables before she quickly assumed that expression of displeasure. Was she angry? There was something that, for a moment, flashed in her eyes and made her cheeks flame before she became aloof again.

What possible reason did *she* have to be angry? He had kept this appointment, despite wishing not to be here. It was he who should be furious.

"Good evening, Louisa. You look lovely tonight. I do hope you will save me a dance later in the evening."

"Of course." Her voice was steady and calm while her fingers played with a silk and ivory fan that dangled from her wrist.

They stood in silence until William finally said, "Cosden has told me I must marry you, Louisa. As a gentleman, I will do so."

"I can tell that you are *enthusiastic* as you consider our union."

"Nonetheless, I have asked you to marry me."

"And yet—" she paused and studied his face for a few seconds, "you ask me, and yet you told me that you would be a terrible husband."

"And so I believe."

"And you said you didn't want to marry."

"This conversation is growing tedious, Lady Louisa," he snapped. "As I said, I will marry you." William attempted to take her hand, but she jerked both behind her back. Why was she behaving like a shrew when he was doing the honorable thing?

"Won't you be seated?" William gestured toward a chair, but she ignored him. It was difficult to propose marriage to a woman who stood and seethed. He would explain that to Cosden when she turned him down. He knew she would reject him.

While Louisa refused to sit, he did, and settled back in a chair to watch her. Not the most courteous of actions.

"You have a low opinion of marriage." She stood a few feet from him and looked down at him, still with the cold expression he couldn't read but which he thought held a trace of temper.

"Not at all. The fact is that in the last few years, since you and I were first acquainted, I have decided marriage is not for me. However"—he held up his hand as she started to speak—"however, if you believe yourself to be ruined beyond recall, then I will marry you."

"How kind of you," she murmured.

"Hardly kind, but not only do I believe it is my duty, but Cosden has threatened bodily harm should I not." He gave a small smile because he was not, after all, the least bit afraid of Cosden. "Although I think him the most tedious of men, he has a reputation with a pistol I would not like to challenge."

"I will not force you to declare yourself," she said frigidly. "However"—she mimicked his word—"however, I am delighted to know that marriage to me is preferable to being shot."

"I apologize for my poor choice of words." He continued to study her, but she didn't speak. She looked not at him but studied her fan instead. He refused to play her game, whatever it was. "If that is the end of our discussion, then I hope you will excuse me."

He stood and turned to leave. He'd just reached for the doorknob when something hit him on the back of the head. Leaning over to pick it up, he saw the object was Louisa's fan. He strode to Louisa and handed it to her. "I believe some bad-tempered shrew threw this at me. I would appreciate you giving it to her, were you to see her."

She took it from him. "Do you understand fan language, my lord?" With a snap, she opened the fan and waved it furiously.

"Louisa," he sighed as he spoke, hoping she would realize how poorly she was acting and how put out he was. "Why are you so angry? I have offered for you and you turned me down. What more am I to do?"

She turned away from him and walked to the mantle where she leaned against a classical frieze.

His friends had often teased him about his golden tongue, a joke he'd never appreciated. Now he felt he had lost his ability to talk to a woman. At least, to talk to this glowering female. Perhaps his desire not to marry had turned his tongue to lead.

"Has your golden tongue turned to lead?" she asked.

"What?"

"My sister tells me," she said as she advanced slowly toward him with a prowling gait he found oddly attractive, "that your golden tongue has won the hearts of many ladies." She stopped but not before he saw pain flash across her face then replaced by anger.

He shook his head. "Louisa, I never attempted to lead you astray in any way, certainly not with what your sister called my *golden tongue.*"

"And why not?"

"Why not?" He shook his head. "Louisa, I always behaved as a gentleman with you."

"Yes."

From her expression and the way she spoke, he got the feeling that his behaving so well bothered her a little.

"Why did you not even attempt to woo me? Why do you have no desire to marry me?" She took several steps toward him, still waving her fan in front of her.

He took a few steps back. "Louisa, I explained that I do not wish to marry. Not to anyone."

"Am I not pretty enough?" she asked taking another step. "Or witty enough? Perhaps you prefer a blond?"

"There is nothing wrong with you."

"Nothing?" She crossed her arms in front of her and fixed her gaze on him.

"There is *nothing* wrong with you. You are very attractive."

"Ahh, attractive." She considered that. "Am I too slender? Or too tall?"

"As I said, there is nothing wrong with you or your . . . your shape." He could not believe he was having this conversation with a lady, and sincerely hoped there was no one outside the door to overhear them. "You are very lovely. In every way."

He stopped, attempting to think of something to say before he remembered the original topic of their conversation. "If I were to marry, you would be as good a choice as anyone. Better, probably. I don't want to marry anyone at all. Not ever."

She didn't say a word but she looked up at him, her beautiful eyes thoughtful. "Thank you. I don't want to marry you either."

"I find you beautiful but—" He realized what she said. "You don't want to marry me?"

"No, I really don't. You are right."

"I am?"

"I believe we would not suit." She moved around him to the door. "I must admit I was not at all happy that you were so very opposed to marrying me. I wondered why you didn't want to marry me, if you found something missing in me."

"Of course not."

"Now I know, I won't allow it to bother me." She nodded. "And I must admit I was curious as to how you would ask me."

"That's it?" He drew himself up to his full height and glared down at her. "You wanted to meet with me, for me to pay my addresses so you could see how I would ask you to marry me?"

She nodded. "You did not do it well. Why you did so poorly confuses me." She tapped her cheek with her fan. "You see, William, I believe you may want to marry me."

"What?"

"William, I believe you're very angry because

Cosden demanded you ask me. That is why you could not do so pleasantly." Louisa paused and thought for a moment.

The blasted woman didn't listen to a word I said. "I thought I asked very pleasant . . ."

"No, neither pleasantly nor passionately." She shook her head. "But I understand, you do not want to do what Cosden tells you to do." She tapped him lightly on the chest with her fan. "I cannot blame you. Cosden has the ability to make one feel like a fool and a failure."

"I most certainly would not behave in such a way." He took hold of the fan and pushed it away from him. "Stop poking me."

She thought before speaking. "But, it's not just Cosden's pushing you, William. I believe you're afraid to take the risk of loving someone."

"I am not afraid of—"

"But I'm not afraid. Because of our wonderful adventure, I'm not going to stay a maiden aunt who lives only through her family."

Louisa smiled absently and sweetly at William as if he was nothing more than a mere acquaintance, and not as if they had raced all over Essex together. Could he also read relief in her expression? Certainly not. "How could you say . . . ?"

"And so, even as you so unwillingly asked me to marry you," she said, "I do thank you."

Poised to finally complete a sentence, he stopped in surprise. "Thank me? Why?"

"Because I discovered that I enjoy being with a man. Oh, I do not mean just your kisses although I found them pleasant."

"Pleasant?" *How could she describe my kisses as merely pleasant?*

"Yes, pleasant." She nodded. "What I appreciate most is that you helped me discover that life is an adventure to be enjoyed and savored, to be lived to the fullest." She smiled and her eyes shone as she flung her arms out. "Now that I have had this experience, I believe I shall begin some interesting . . . oh, what shall I call them? Flirtations? Liaisons?"

He almost choked. "What? You are not planning to take a lover, Louisa!" He could feel the veins in his neck tightening. His voice became louder than it should be during a polite conversation but, devil take it, this was hardly a polite conversation.

"I don't know. Perhaps." She twinkled up at him. "I may be too innocent for that although I daresay I could find someone to teach me. Perhaps my sisters could tell me . . ."

"You cannot do that! You are not like women who . . . not like that kind of woman."

She ignored him. After studying herself in the mirror, she twirled toward him and asked, "Do I look all right?"

"You look fine."

"Thank you for teaching me about myself." She started toward the door, then turned back to him. "I believe I am going to enjoy myself much more. I will do a great deal more dancing and flirting and kissing." Those lips that made such outrageous comments touched her gloved hand then waved to him.

"What do you mean?" he bellowed behind her. "I didn't teach you to kiss so you could kiss other men." He took her arm, pulled her close to him and scowled down at her. "All right, Louisa, will you marry me?"

"My understanding is that you do not want to marry." She wiggled her arm from his grasp.

"That is true."

"For goodness sake, William, I do not want to marry someone who doesn't want to marry. What more do we have to discuss?"

She looked at him with eyes wide and innocent and more beautiful than he remembered.

"Now, if you'll excuse me," she said. "I plan to look at eligible men with new eyes, with a completely different outlook. Perhaps there will be a man out there I can fall in love with, one who wants to marry me, a man who does believe in love."

Before she could open the door, he threw himself against it. "There aren't any. Men don't. They'll make pretty speeches and swear to love you forever but all they want are your kisses. I know. I'm a man."

"It could be that they're not all like you. Perchance I will give a few kisses away and see." She pushed him away from the door, opened it, and left the parlor.

"I liked Miss Prim better!" he shouted after her.

He wouldn't have thought her refusal would hurt anything more than his pride, but as he watched her move away with a seductive sway in her walk, he realized he had tossed away what he really wanted. He'd chased away a beautiful woman who was loving, loyal and strong; a woman who had ridden with him to save the baby and had never complained when she was in pain or tired and hungry; a woman who had saved his life, as much as he hated to admit it.

She truly was as beautiful inside as out. And strong all the way through.

As the door slammed behind her, to his great surprise he was filled with the same pain he'd experienced when her father had rejected his request to marry Louisa, when he'd had to ride off without seeing her again.

And in that moment, the certainty hit him like a hundred bricks. He really did want to marry Louisa.

Fool! He'd allowed Cosden, memories of his parents' marriage to . . . no, he couldn't blame Louisa's rejection on anyone else but himself. He had allowed his own cowardice and stiff-necked pride to make a muddle of the entire thing.

And knowing Louisa as he did, she would not make it easy for him to press his suit again.

Chapter Twelve

What happened, William wondered as he opened the door Louisa had closed behind her. The woman had not only spurned his offer of marriage, but she behaved as if he had introduced her to a whole new world of pleasure which she planned to plunge into, but without him. And, wearing that gown, she would have no trouble finding a man, many men, willing to dive into that world with her. To make it worse, she had made him her confidant about her future liaisons.

It irritated him. Greatly.

He stepped into the corridor and followed Louisa into the large parlor where the entire company gathered. After nodding to Fothergill and Bradenton, he looked for Louisa and spied her talking—no, the hussy was flirting—with Hampton. Didn't she know anything? Of course she didn't! She'd trusted *him*, hadn't she? Innocent as a babe but now chatting with Hampton, her eyes flashing, her eyelashes fluttering.

She certainly wasn't his Miss Prim anymore. Not that she'd ever been *his* Miss Prim but, at this moment, he couldn't think logically. Right now, he wanted to call Hampton out.

Blast it, the man was examining Louisa, and half the men in the parlor envied him. The reason the rest of the men were not ogling Louisa's charms was that they hadn't seen her yet. He could not allow this! He had to teach her discretion. He owed her that.

William headed for the lovely Hepplewhite chairs where Hampton and Louisa sat and laughed together, when someone put a hand on his arm and stopped him. William turned to see Julianna, who attempted to pull him away from Louisa. The duchess grasped his arm with a strength he'd not realized was within her. Finally he was forced to stop and turn.

"Tell me, Woodstone, how is your family?"

"My parents and brother are deceased. My sister is married. I haven't seen her for a long time." He twisted away and started back across the room but she reached for his arm again.

"Come with me." She took his hand in an iron grip and pulled him toward a deserted corner. "Did you ask my sister to marry you?" she whispered.

"Yes," he growled, keeping his eyes on Louisa and attempting to free himself from the duchess' powerful grip without tossing her to the carpet.

"From the way you two are acting, I can only guess she refused." When he didn't deign to answer, Julianna continued. "Why did she refuse? I thought she liked you well enough."

"According to your sister, neither affection nor honor are reasons to marry." He again pulled away from Julianna's hand but the duchess kept a firm hold.

"Is that all?"

"No, but is it necessary for me to air all our dirty laundry here and now?"

"Yes, Woodstone, it is. Remember, I witnessed a great deal of dirty laundry from the adventure the two of you had, alone. I am Louisa's sister. What happened when you proposed?"

"She refused me."

Julianna glared at him. "I would like a few details. What did you say?"

"I told her I asked only because it was my duty and Cosden forced me to do so."

"How charming."

"Then she said she didn't want to marry me. It was very amicable."

"Ahh, I can tell you made a great effort to charm her. However, if you do not suit, we will attempt to keep the scandal between us. Please stay away from her," she ordered before putting her arm through his and dragging him after her. "I would like you to meet our neighbor, Lady Helena."

"We have met." William nodded toward the viscountess.

"Dinner will be served shortly, and you escort the viscountess. In fact, I see the footman coming to announce dinner now." She placed the viscountess' hand on his arm, then went to the front of the line to stand with her husband.

"And how is Humphries?" William asked politely.

"Not well. Fell. Off his horse. Hunting."

He'd forgotten Lady Helena's habit of short, incomplete sentences and had to listen carefully to understand her. He could see Louisa at the left hand of her brother-in-law, next to Godwell, who was holding a spirited conversation with her.

"Idiot man is going to drop his meal down the front of her dress," he mumbled.

"Beg pardon?"

With great effort, William forced his attention away from Louisa and to his dining partner. "My lady, I hear you have a new stud in your stable."

She was off on a staccato description of the new horse until the next course was served, and he turned toward the dinner partner on his left.

William noted that Godwell did not converse with the woman on his left. William could not blame him. The Baroness Pardue was a haughty woman who had no love for rakehells like Godwell. However, it was her duty to demand his attention, to force his attentions away from an innocent like Louisa. For she was an innocent, a lamb who truly did not know what men wanted. For a few seconds, he considered ordering the baroness to talk to Godwell until he decided Julianna would not consider this correct.

He looked around the table. Every unmarried man and many of the married ones were aware of the allure that emanated from Louisa. He had changed her into a seductress, and she had no understanding of the consequences. He watched her look up at Godwell through her wonderfully thick eyelashes. When Louisa chuckled at something the idiot said, a becoming pink covered her cheeks.

William groaned.

"Excuse me? Did you say something?"

William looked at his conversation partner, a sweet young lady who, he guessed, was just out of the schoolroom. Poor child to have drawn him as her dinner partner.

"I am Mary Logan, the squire's daughter."

"Do you often come to parties here?" William asked politely.

"Oh, no. This is my first formal party ever."

Then Godwell whispered in Louisa's ear.

"Did you say something?" Miss Logan asked.

"No, merely clearing my throat."

"I asked if you had visited Cosden Park, and you

assumed a gruff expression." She shivered. "I thought you growled."

"Please excuse me. My journey here was somewhat difficult and I am still rattled. No, I have not visited the park before although I do know the duke and his duchess from London."

"And her grace's sister? You know her from London?"

"I knew her in the past, but I have not seen her in many years. Why do you ask?"

"Well, I just wondered. Please excuse me if I speak out of turn, but I am young and very new at dinner conversation. You seem inordinately interested in her."

"Oh?" His left eyebrow lifted.

"You keep your eyes on her at all times."

"How could I watch her when I have such a lovely dinner partner? Tell me about your home." As Miss Logan spoke, he attended her words so closely the child began to stammer.

Nor was the ball much better. He had asked Louisa for a dance, and she promised him one, only one. He danced once with Miss Logan and once with Julianna. During the rest of the evening, he lounged against a marble pillar and kept his eyes on Louisa. Just, of course, to protect her from predators. He thought she did not notice him, but, if she did, she ignored the warning glances he sent her.

On her part, Louisa danced with every eligible man

and many who were not, in his opinion. All were entranced by her. He knew why. He closed his eyes so he wouldn't lose his temper and gripped one hand tightly with the other to keep himself from beating every one of her partners. When he opened his eyes again, Cosden stood before him.

"Let's play cards," Cosden suggested, at the same time taking William's arm and urging him toward the card room.

"I did not remember either you or your wife were such strong, determined people," William remonstrated. "The duchess seized me before dinner and here you are, forcing me to the card room where I do not want to go."

"The duchess and I wish to save Louisa's reputation. You watch her as if you are about to devour her. It certainly gives people an odd opinion of your relationship. They wonder about your reason for such a great interest in Louisa, and I will not have her harmed further." He pulled William from the ballroom.

"People also must think it very odd that you and I are struggling," William said.

"Then don't resist me." Cosden dropped William's arm.

"I, too, wish to keep Louisa's reputation unblemished. That is why I am keeping an eye on these young bucks."

"Oh, is that what you are doing?"

"Yes, what did you think I was doing?"

"I do not usually speak in this manner. In fact there are many who would consider me a bore, but I must make this explicit." Cosden cleared his throat and tugged at his neckcloth. "Woodstone, you look as if you are a male dog, and Louisa is the only female in heat." He put his handkerchief to his nose and sniffed into it.

"Cosden!"

"I told you it was unrefined but there it is." Cosden patted his forehead with the handkerchief. "You are not helping her. People are talking about your surveillance of her."

"My what? I am merely trying to make sure she's not taken advantage of by the scoundrels you have invited here."

"They are hardly scoundrels. These young men are the pick of society and would not dare to give Louisa a slip on the shoulder while *I* am around to protect her. Any one of them would make a fine husband for Louisa. Since you have chosen not to marry her, you have no say in what Louisa does."

"I . . ."

Cosden glared. "Woodstone, I warn you to stay away from Louisa. Do not make her conspicuous."

"I wouldn't do that. I am fond of Louisa."

"Then leave her alone, Woodstone. Do not scare off men who would be her husband. We are delighted to see her display an interest in marriage. She will make a fine wife and mother."

"If her husband isn't inclined to murder her," William mumbled.

"I beg your pardon?"

"She is out there, nearly naked, and flirting with every rake." William held his hand up to stop Cosden's interruption. "I know, they are fine young men. Nonetheless, she's flirting outrageously with them and doesn't know what they have in mind."

"In the first place, Louisa is wearing a dress that belongs to my wife whom I do *not* allow to attend balls practically naked." Cosden glared at William. "Nor is Louisa flirting outrageously. She's behaving just as she should. The fact that she looks very lovely and men admire her is not immoral."

"You are correct, Cosden. I'll bother her no more after our one dance. Perhaps I should leave in the morning."

"If you do that, her reputation might never recover. No, you must stay and behave like a gentleman! Dance with other women. Join with the other guests, but leave Louisa alone."

"Yes, your grace." William stifled his anger. It was galling, but Cosden was right again.

After a few hands of cards, he returned to the ballroom to claim his dance with Louisa. "Are you enjoying yourself this evening?" He bowed before her.

"Yes, I am, thank you."

"You stated you didn't plan to marry because men expect you to be an empty-headed simpleton, and yet you seem to be flirting with every man in sight. Have you changed your mind?"

"I have, I believe," she said as the music brought them together again. "I was much too serious and unrealistic when I was young."

"Good Lord, Louisa," he burst out, then forced himself to speak more quietly. "You were serious about love and marriage only a few days ago."

Louisa smiled up at him, then looked at the other swirling couples. "Yes, isn't it amazing how life changes?"

They danced in silence for a few moments until she whispered, "What do you think of Hampton?"

"What do you mean?"

"He seems like a nice person," she said as she placed her hand on his arm. "Is he?"

"He is a rogue and a womanizer."

"Oh." Louisa looked around the room. "What about—"

"They are all rogues and womanizers. All men are. None of those men are right for you."

As the music came to an end, he escorted her to her next partner. "Thank you for the information." She smiled up at him.

Unsmiling and with his brows drawn in a V, William turned on his heels and returned to the card room.

He was behaving himself, Louisa thought with a touch of disappointment. While he glared at her as her partners swirled her around the ballroom, she'd felt an altogether unworthy pleasure in his vigilance. It caused quite a stir, a reaction the very proper Louisa had never experienced but which the new Louisa found glorious. In fact, it almost assuaged the pain his lack of interest in marriage to her had caused.

"What is the matter with Woodstone?" Fothergill asked her as they awaited the start of the music. "I've never seen him like this. He's mooning around like a rejected suitor and watching you."

"We knew each other as children and met again recently." She hid her face behind her fan. "I dare not say more."

"Poor fellow. You must have broken his heart."

"Oh, certainly not that, sir. But you were telling me about your recent visit to Bath. Pray continue."

The next morning, William only nodded when Louisa entered the breakfast parlor. He left with a group to explore a cathedral while she joined the younger set on a picnic. "As a chaperone," she'd said, only to be teased about her great age by Hampton and Fothergill who joined her, pretending to be members of the younger set themselves. Then she returned to Cosden Park and played with Julianna's sons.

While Louisa entertained her nephews, William gathered Godwell, Fothergill, and Bradenton, his friends from the Home Office, to the library to discuss what had happened with Bea. He believed he could trust these men but did not tell them where the child was. He asked the three men to return to London and to make every effort to find who had told the French where the baby was. William would stay at Cosden Park to see what developed.

"Two of you must stay at the office at all times until I get back," William said. "Until our spy can return to England and gather his family together safely."

When the three left, William attempted to avoid Julianna's eye. Another thing for her to hate him for: Destroying the balance at her table with the departure of his friends.

When Boswell arrived that afternoon, she gave Louisa a scold while she hung her clothing. "What were you thinking, running off like that?" Boswell turned toward her, frowning. "When are you getting married?"

"I'm not getting married, Boswell."

"You're not getting married, my lady?" Boswell fixed her mistress with the glare only a servant of long-standing was allowed to give.

"Please keep this secret. So few know what happened that my reputation should be safe."

Boswell shook her head. "Running around all over the country, alone with a man, why aren't you getting married?"

"He doesn't want to marry me. He asked me only because Cosden told him he had to."

"And you turned him down?" Boswell gasped.

"Boswell, I cannot marry a man who doesn't love me."

"Romantic nonsense. Well, don't you come to me expecting me to . . ." Unable to think of a completion to the sentence, she continued to hang the dresses.

"Boswell, I won't. I have learned my lesson. Please forgive me for my folly."

The old retainer harrumphed in reply.

It was late the next afternoon when Louisa came downstairs from the nursery to see William in the hallway speaking with a new arrival. She paused, not wishing to intrude, but realized tea would be served shortly, and she would allow nothing to keep her from the lovely treats Cosden's chef prepared.

When she entered the front hall, William turned and said, "Ahh, Lady Louisa, I would like you to meet my good friend, the Marquis of Lasington."

The man turned toward Louisa, his gray eyes studying her. "Good day, Lady Louisa," he said in a deep voice.

Louisa drew back from the marquis and placed a hand on her chest. It was he. She recognized his voice and those cold, piercing gray eyes. Oh, they weren't cold now. They looked friendly and warm, but she knew what they could look like. She knew this was the man who'd looked through the leaves while she hid from the pursuers, and coolly ordered Green to find them and kill them.

Lasington looked puzzled as she leaped away from

him. "My lady?" he asked in that deep, easy-to-recognize voice.

"What is wrong with you?" William asked as she almost cowered against the wall.

Louisa struggled to hide her terror. "I don't know what happened. I stepped on something that threw me off balance. How clumsy of me." She glanced at the floor for a moment as if to search for that imaginary something, then gave both men a brilliant smile and slipped her arm through William's. "Are you gentlemen coming to tea now?"

"Not now." William attempted to push Louisa away, but she refused to loosen her grip. "I will wait until Lasington has found his chamber and will show him the way to the parlor."

After the marquis disappeared up the steps behind a footman, William turned to Louisa. "What is the matter with your family? All of you keep grabbing me."

"I have to talk to you." Louisa glanced around the hall. There were too many people gathering to speak privately so she pulled him toward the study. "Alone! This is important."

"Most certainly not, Louisa. I have been ordered to leave you alone." He grasped her hand, tossed it from his arm, and followed the marquis up the stairs. She stood there in disbelief.

That evening, while some of the guests entertained the others with theatrics, Louisa attempted to get

William's attention, but he ignored her. When she noticed a few of the guests staring at her, she attempted to be more subtle in her efforts but to no avail. He still refused to look at her.

The entire time, she knew exactly where Lasington was. He acted as if he was no different from the other guests. Once he glanced at her, his eyes as cold as she remembered, then he looked away quickly. Had she not known he was evil, she might not have noticed the look. Did he guess she'd recognized him? The thought frightened her terribly. However, she lost sight of him before the tea tray was brought in and was able to relax for awhile.

After the guests yawned and turned toward their rooms, Louisa still had not been able to talk to William. Julianna had pulled her aside and told her to stop pursuing Woodstone and to act like a lady, and Cosden glared at her. Louisa did not care.

Although she followed William to his chambers, she was unable to enter due to the guests in the hallway. Frustrated, she went to her own suite and sent Boswell away, receiving a lecture about her hoydenish behavior before her dresser left.

Louisa waited until the halls were silent. Cautiously, she opened her door and looked up and down the corridor. Empty. She left her room and closed the door softly behind her. Staying against the wall and in the shadow, she tiptoed around the corner, down another hallway, and to William's door. Without knocking, she opened it, hoping he was alone. She slipped inside.

Wearing a long blue robe over his unmentionables, he sat reading, his profile silhouetted against the light of a lamp. A thin curl of smoke twisted around his head from the cigarillo he held. At least he was alone and dressed, she thought relieved.

"Hello," she said.

"What the . . . ?" He leaped to his feet, obviously on the defense against an intruder. He relaxed when he saw her but that turned to exasperation. "Louisa, why are you here? I have been behaving honorably. Are you trying to ruin yourself?"

"I needed to talk to you. You refused."

"At the expressed request of your sister and her husband. Now," he said grasping her shoulders, turning her around, and pushing her toward the door. When he reached to open it, the cigarillo almost burned her. "Go!"

Wresting herself away from him, she moved back into the center of the room. "I'll not go until you heed me. If you insist on pushing me out, I will pound on your door and scream. Then Cosden will most assuredly call you out. You must listen. This is not nonsense."

He dropped his hands and looked at her as if she was the Medusa until, little by little, his expression softened. "Do you need to talk about how badly I proposed and behaved yesterday?" He reached out his hand and touched her cheek. "Louisa, I'm sorry. I behaved like a fool. Are you here to forgive me?" He placed the cigarillo on a table next to the door. "You were right. I am afraid."

"I was right?" she whispered, amazed.

"Do you forgive me?" At her nod, William put his arms around her and lowered his lips.

"William," she said breathlessly. "I have something important to tell you."

"Later."

She hated to do it, but she lifted his head and met his eyes. "William, this is about the spies."

"What?" Suddenly alert and professional, he moved away from her but kept his gaze on her face. "Tell me."

"Do you remember that I saw a man with gray eyes looking at me through the trees? And that I heard his voice?"

"Yes."

"That man is your friend, the marquis."

"Lasington? Are you sure?"

"Of course I'm sure. Do you think I came here just to cuddle?"

He ground his cigarillo out and walked toward the window in thought. Slowly he turned to face her across the room. "You said you saw only his eyes. Did you see his face?"

"No."

"How can you be sure?"

"I told you I'd never forget those eyes." She shuddered. "Or his voice. You must admit, he has a very distinctive voice. Much lower than most men's."

William considered her words.

"Does he have access to the information about the spy?" she asked.

"Louisa, I can't believe—"

"Does he have access to that information?"

"Yes, he has a position at the Home Office. It would be easy for him to find out whatever he wants, but I can't believe it. We served on the peninsula together." For almost a minute he seemed to forget she was there, so lost was he in thought. Finally he looked up at her, surprised she was still there. "Oh, Louisa. Thank you for telling me."

"What will you do?"

"I don't know. We'll discuss this tomorrow, but tonight we have to get you out of this room without anyone seeing you." He led her toward the door. "Stay behind me." After looking out into the hallway, he said, "The hall is clear. Go on." He pushed her in the back and silently closed the door behind her.

Not completely satisfied with the outcome of her visit—although she couldn't say why not—Louisa returned to her room without seeing anyone and began to prepare for bed.

Was Lasington still here? Probably not. He must have sensed that, somehow, she'd recognized him. Someone should check his room, to see if he'd left. Oh, not her, of course. The man frightened her enough she never wanted to be alone with him. Perhaps she should go back to see if William was going to look for Lasington, but she guessed he'd do that in the morning.

What would William do with the information she'd given him? It would be necessary to get it to London immediately, to arrest the marquis and destroy the spy ring as soon as possible.

As soon as possible. Immediately. She repeated those words to herself and remembered William's quick decision and haste when they'd left Longtrees. From his past behavior, she knew he wouldn't put it off. He'd leave now, immediately, to get to London as soon as possible.

Good heavens, he'd said they would discuss this tomorrow, but the man was lying to her.

Certainly he would not leave without her. Would he? Yes, he would, although she'd made it clear they worked together.

He'd pushed her out of the room. He'd contemplated the situation for a moment, had probably made a quick decision that didn't include her, and shoved her out of his room. Yes, he would leave without her. He might have already gone.

With a quick movement, she buttoned her gown again then grabbed her shoes as she stepped into the dark hallway and ran toward his bedroom, heedless of the reaction of anyone who might be in the corridor.

Chapter Thirteen

"William," Louisa muttered as she stumbled down the stairs in the dark. "If the spies don't get you first, *I* am going to do real harm to you."

She'd gone to his chambers first. They were empty.

She wished she knew where Lasington's suite was. Even as frightened of him as she was, she would have looked there to check on Lasington before concluding William had gone after the man without her. She only hoped she could reach the stables before William left.

Bemoaning the loss of time, she threw her shoes on the floor of the entry and stepped into them, knowing she'd need to wear them on the gravel driveway. Not that the thin soles were much protection she realized once she was outside. She bit her lip as she hurried down the drive with the tiny stones biting into her feet.

For a moment, she ran down the verge, but her feet slipped on the grass. Curse the delay!

"He'll be gone. He's going to be gone by the time I get there," she muttered as she ran. Her breathing became labored and her side hurt, but Louisa didn't pause.

When she saw a dim light shining from the stable, she tried to run even faster. She was gasping for breath when she burst into the building. William had his foot in the stirrup.

"Stop!" she shouted and leaped in front of the dancing horse.

Charger didn't flinch, but William scowled and shouted at her, "You idiot, the horse could have killed you! What are you doing here?" he demanded as he swung into his saddle. "Go back to bed, Louisa. You are not needed."

She stood in the door of the stable, feet wide so he couldn't take Charger past her. "Why are you leaving now? Where are you going?"

"Come, come, Louisa. You wouldn't be here if you didn't know where I'm going. I'm going to London, of course." His voice resounded with authority. "And you are not coming with me. I have the situation under control."

"The marquis' horse is gone, my lord." The stable-boy spoke as he came from the back wing of the stable.

"Then he has already left." Louisa shook her head in frustration.

"Yes, Ivory looked in his bedroom. He wasn't there. Now his horse is gone." William attempted to calm his horse as it danced close to Louisa. "Move, Louisa. I can ride Charger over you. You know I must get this information to the Home Office."

"How long ago did he leave?" she asked the stableboy.

"I don't know, my lady. He must have saddled the horse himself. I was asleep until the viscount yelled for me."

"He knew." She shook her head. "At least, he guessed from my reaction that I recognized him. Or maybe he's just very careful."

"Yes, I believe he probably assumed you recognized him when you almost fainted."

"Hearing his voice was very unexpected."

"Louisa, it wasn't just your response. I did something that probably made him suspicious as well. I told him I'd sent Fothergill, Godwell and Bradenton back to London."

"Did you tell Lasington why you were doing that?"

"Fortunately I didn't have time." William soothed Charger who wanted his head.

"Why do you think Lasington joined the house party? Had he planned to be here or was it because the men who were following us lost us in this area?"

"Louisa, this is hardly the time for a conversation." When she didn't move, he went on. "With his position in society, Lasington knows your sister lives in the vicinity. It may have been a coincidence but I believe it was a good guess on his part. As for arriving without an invitation, the man is welcome everywhere."

Louisa thought for a moment. "He knows you're here without the baby. He has men all around looking for you, just like they were before, but he knows where you are now and he knows where you're going." She looked up at him. "William, you won't get near the Home Office. He'll have you killed before you can tell anyone who the spy is."

"You're being overly dramatic."

"Or he might torture you to find out where Bea is."

He didn't answer, just loosened Charger's reins slightly as the horse fidgeted. "Louisa, get out of my way."

Of course she didn't. "He has hours of head start. He'll have a plan set up by now."

"Hours of head start," William agreed. "That's why I have to go now, Louisa. He left the card room before ten, over four hours ago. Even at night, if he pushed his horse, he'll be in London by now. Lord only knows what schemes he's set in motion."

"Don't you think he's put men all around here?" She turned in a circle. "Men waiting for you along the road? Once they take care of you, they'll come here for me."

"That may be. I'll try to bring help from London."

"But, until then, Cosden will have to protect me and the entire house party."

"I'd not like to go up against Cosden and his pistols, but I don't believe he and the other men could hold off

Lasington's men. The spies are killers without principles." He ran his hand down Charger's neck. "First, I need to go down to the road, to see if there are men stationed there. Move away, Louisa."

Recognizing the futility of attempting to reason with William, she moved to the side, and he rode off.

If there were no guards, William would go on to London. She knew he wouldn't come back for her. If guards had been set, if they saw him, they would capture or kill him. If he didn't come back, she would not know if he was alive or dead. If she were to follow him, they would kill her also, but she had to go. There had to be a backup to make sure the information got to London.

She paced back and forth on the narrow path by the stable, and looked down the drive every few seconds. With every sound, she leaped, then glanced around to find what had made the noise. But she was alone. The groom had gone to bed.

William hadn't returned yet.

It was an eternal wait.

When he finally rode back, William was silent and somber. "There are two men guarding the entrance to the road. They are not my men." He dismounted and tied the reins to a post.

As she paced on the drive, something nagged at her, a memory from her childhood, but it took a minute for her to dredge up. When she did, she raced back to William. "I know another way out of here. It's between the lake and the cliff. I'll show you."

"You are not coming with me, Louisa."

"Then I will go alone. Besides, you will never find the other way out unless I lead you. It is not easy to find."

"I will ask Cosden."

"William, no matter what you do, I will still go to London, without you if necessary. You cannot tie me up to keep me here. One of us must get there." She glared at his set face. "Besides, he doesn't know where it is."

"Louisa, I would worry about you."

"Wouldn't you be more worried if I were out there alone?"

"As much as you enjoyed your earlier adventure, Louisa, this is hardly a romp," he warned, his voice harsh. "As far as Lasington knows, you and I are the only ones who know he works for the French. He will kill you, after he tortures you. That is not something I wish to consider."

"William, we could already have told everyone at the house party. Everyone could be in danger."

"Yes, and that concerns me. I must discuss this with Cosden." He shook his head. "I don't like this, Louisa. Not at all, but I see no solution. You will need to come with me to show me the other way out unless I can convince Cosden to come."

"Yes, William." She lowered her head to hide her smile. "I don't believe Cosden will leave his estate to chase spies."

"I don't either." William turned toward the house.

"And don't try to fool me. You're delighted." William turned to the stableboy who came into the yard yawning. "Keep Charger ready to go. I'll return shortly." Then he took Louisa's arm. "Let's talk."

They walked to a bench next to the drive and sat. "Why not a boat across the lake? Certainly I could find a mount on the other side."

"There is a scenic waterfall on the south side. Although it's safe to fish and sail close to this side, there is a dangerous undertow further from the shore. Years ago, the heir of an earlier duke died when his boat went over it."

He thought for a moment but couldn't seem to come up with another answer. "All right. I'll tell the stableboy to saddle Bess." That completed, they walked to the mansion.

"Do you think the spies could be on the estate already, hiding?" Louisa attempted to peer through the darkness.

"I doubt it. I believe they will stay on the road. Why come onto the estate with all the people here when they only want you and me?"

The idea she was one of two targets made Louisa shiver. No, this was not a romp.

He walked faster. "Return to your chambers and pack a few things. I will meet you in the stable, although I have no idea how long the conversation with Cosden will take."

"Do not tell Cosden I am coming with you," she

warned. "If you do, you may have to ask me to marry you again."

"And you may turn me down, as usual."

When they got to the mansion, they parted: Louisa to change into a riding habit and write a note for her sister while William talked to Cosden about the problem.

The habit she chose was brown and, although fashionable, it was very plain, the simplest and most basic item of her wardrobe.

If she encountered any of the three men she'd met in that earlier encounter in Wimberton, did she look different enough from Mrs. Boggs to deceive anyone? She hoped she did. After all, this time her face was clean, and her hair neatly combed. She looked every inch a lady. If the spies found them, she could tilt her face down, chin close to her chest so only the feather on the top of her hat could be seen.

Of course, they would recognize William. When they did, they would most certainly be highly suspicious of a woman riding with him alone in the middle of the night. No, wearing clean clothing and holding her head differently would not disguise her. They'd have to ride hard and hope they'd not run into the traitors. If they ran into Lasington, no disguise would save either of them.

Louisa threw a few things into a small case, pulled on her gloves and went to the door. For a moment, the realization of what they were about to do frightened her so much she couldn't breathe. With bravado, she tossed her head and said to herself, "I'm off now." The she whispered, "May God watch over us."

She waited in the stable yard for almost half an hour. When she first got there, she checked to see that Charger was still in the stable. He was. She paced then sat, then she paced again.

And she worried. It was getting so late and Lasington had such a long head start on them. He would have had plenty of time to set up roadblocks between here and London.

The sun would rise in a few hours, and here they were, still at Cosden Park.

"Are you ready to go?" William shouted when he saw her from the corner of the house.

"Of course. What kept you?"

"Cosden wanted to know everything and would not stop asking questions." He signaled for the groom to bring their horses. "I told him you were coming with me."

She sighed. "What did he say?"

"I promised I would keep you safe."

"He accepted it?" She took Bess' bridle.

"I told him about the great danger if there was a spy at Cosden Park. I said your presence would put everyone there in terrible jeopardy." He took the case and tied it to his saddle. "Cosden was quite upset about it, upset enough to tell me to take you immediately. To keep *you* safe, of course."

"So Cosden has washed his hands of me to protect himself?"

"Oh, not only for himself. I am sure he wished to protect his family but was perfectly willing to sacrifice you."

"I wash my hands of him, too," she huffed. Although she was glad Cosden had not demanded she stay, it would be nice to be less expendable.

She put her foot in the groom's hand to allow him to toss her on Bess' back then settled herself on the ladies' saddle. It felt so much more comfortable and steady to her than riding astride.

At the same time, William mounted. He kicked Charger and took off before he realized Louisa needed to be in the lead. As he allowed her in front of him, he said, "I hope the spies have not found this entrance. I would hate to run into them."

"Although they may be on the road, I don't believe they could know this road. It is so seldom used the opening is very overgrown."

"How do you know about it?"

"Our family has visited Cosden Park for years. When I was a child, I had the run of the grounds. This was one of my favorite rides."

They rode in silence, afraid that their voices would carry on the breeze. Louisa concentrated on trying to remember the twists and turns in the dark. Only a short distance before the place where the trail met the road, Louisa turned to William. "We're almost there," she whispered.

"Wait here," he said. "I'll see if there is anyone ahead. Do not move until I call you."

Slowly and as quietly as possible, William moved through the branches that hid the lane from the road. He was gone only a minute before Louisa heard a man shout, "Halt! Who goes there?"

Chapter Fourteen

For an endless minute, no other sounds came from the road but the words hung in the air. Louisa wanted to do something, to ride out, to save William but what would she do? Anything she did might make the situation worse. Besides, if something was to happen to William— *oh, please no!*—she would have to ride to London.

When Bess shuffled a little, Louisa feared that whoever was on the road would hear that, would know there was another person there.

"Hello," she heard William mumble, his words slurred as if he'd been drinking. "Why don't you halt yourself." He laughed inanely.

"I have instructions to stop anyone on this road, sir. Who are you and what are you doing here at this hour?"

"Who are you and what are *you* doing here at this hour?" William laughed again.

Then she heard the sound of a hand slapping something.

"Why'd you do that?" William whimpered. "I'm not doing anything." After a pause, he said, "You in the Army? Used to be in the Army. Not what I wanted but I'm a patriot, served my country on the peninsula." He began a wandering story about some battle.

"Who are you and what are you doing here?" the man repeated. "We're looking for a dangerous criminal who might be on this road."

Then Louisa heard a hollow sound, as if someone had tapped on a melon, followed by the sound of someone falling off a horse. After almost a minute, William said, "Come on, Louisa. It should be safe now."

"Are you hurt?"

He didn't answer.

On the road, Louisa saw a man unconscious on the ground. William had dismounted and stood watching him.

"I hit him with my gun. Don't know what to do with him now." He glanced up at Louisa. "I'd prefer not to kill him but he'll soon wake up and tell the others I was here. I have nothing to tie him up with."

"My petticoat, William." She picked up her skirt and began tearing lengths of material from the garment. "This should keep him still for a while."

"How handy petticoats are. They have so many uses, perhaps men should start wearing them."

She smiled as she handed the first lacy strip to William and watched him bind the man's hands with it.

"Why do you think this man was here? I didn't think anyone else knew about this drive."

He used the second strip to tie the spy's feet. "Pure bad luck, I think. He was patrolling the road when I came out." He tied another strip across the spy's mouth. "But it shows us how quickly Lasington worked to try to keep us out of London."

Yes, guards at the entrance to Cosden Park and patrols on the road. Lasington must have a huge organization to get this surveillance set up so quickly.

With Lasington's men in place, how would she and William get the information to Whitehall?

Finished tying up the man, William slung the man over his shoulder and carried him into the woods. When he came back, he slapped the rump of the spy's horse and watched it gallop away before mounting Charger. He then lightly kicked Charger and started off, in the opposite direction from London.

"Where are we going?" said Louisa as she raced Bess to keep up with him.

"After seeing what's outside Cosden Park, I'm sure the road between here and London will be heavily patrolled."

Louisa nodded.

"That's why I decided to turn away from London, to

drive a wide loop and come back further north to enter the city. I hope Lasington's men are located between here and London, that he doesn't have more to deploy in other directions, on other highways."

"Ahh, I see. I imagine you learned that sort of subterfuge from your experiences on the peninsula and in the Home Office."

Without a word, he began to ride hard with Louisa pushing Bess behind him.

While they rode, she listened for horses behind them but heard nothing. After almost an hour, the rain began. At first, it came in a light sprinkle but got harder quickly, until it was falling in sheets which made it difficult to see even a few feet ahead of them. As the road became slippery and muddy, William slowed the pace.

To make the trip worse, the temperature fell with the storm. Louisa was more miserable than she'd been on their first ride. Rain poured the length of the brim of her once fashionable hat and down her neck while mud splattered her face and habit.

For a while she wondered if she was better off with the hat or without it. It *did* keep her head dry but dumped water down her back. The problem resolved itself when the weight of water collapsed the brim and spilled water all over her already waterlogged body while the feathers drooped into her eyes. She tossed the entire mess on the road.

Not a great loss, but now she had nothing to protect her from the deluge and the gusting wind that tugged at her hair. In addition, the tempest blew cold rain up the skirt of her habit while muddy water splashed over boots that were not nearly as thick and warm as she had hoped.

Still, William rode ahead of her, tall and straight in the saddle as if the conditions didn't bother him in the least.

Blast the man!

She dared not complain or ask him to slow down or she would land at an inn or on someone's estate while he trotted to London.

When an enormous splash of mud hit her in the face, she realized she'd allowed herself to get too close to Charger. She pulled Bess back and settled into the rhythm Bess had established. The pounding of rain sounded like a fusillade. Thunder had become a cannon blast which made Bess prance in fear.

After another hour, William slowed down.

"Let's allow the horses to rest a little." He pulled to the side of the road and let them drink from a puddle of clean water. "We're not making good time." He shook his head before looking at Louisa, obviously noticing the mud dripping down her face. "How are you doing?"

She pulled up the skirt of her habit to wipe at the mess. "Don't worry about me. A little water won't stop me." *Oh, please, don't send me away.*

"I never thought otherwise. You are one of the bravest people I have ever known."

"How could you think that?" she asked, surprised.

"I'm just a maiden aunt who's trying to help her country but keeps ending up in difficult situations."

"That's exactly why. Most maiden aunts are content to sit and sew and gossip, but you are game for this, even though you know the danger. Bravery isn't lack of fear; it's doing what has to be done, in spite of fear."

"But you know true bravery. You've fought in war."

"That's why I recognize courage, Louisa."

As the wind picked up a little, rain began to fall even harder. "The road doesn't seem to be affected yet," William observed.

"How much more water can it take?"

"We'll find that out as we ride." Without another word, he pulled on the reins and turned Charger back to the road. For the next hour, they pounded down the road, slowing every time the rain and wind increased.

William hated this. Hated that Louisa rode behind him, not complaining, convinced they were comrades in arms while he wished she was safe and warm somewhere else. Then the rain came down with such force he could not see. He drew Charger to a halt, worried the horse could slip or step into a hole.

As he sat there, he heard the pounding of hoofs behind them, horses coming fast as if in pursuit. William grabbed Bess' bridle and led her off the road and into the forest. They listened as the riders came closer. It seemed an eternity as Louisa and he waited, as the sounds drew nearer.

"Is it they? Is it the traitors?" she whispered.

At first, William didn't answer. He listened, his body taut and still. "I don't know." He watched two horsemen race past and thought it probably was the spies. Who else would be out here, riding all out in this weather? Only people with a great deal to lose or much to gain. They waited a few minutes before William led them back onto the road. Again, they traveled in silence until he saw a small inn.

"Let's stop here for a while. The horses need to rest, and so do we." They tossed the reins to the groom then went inside to procure a private parlor and a luncheon. Only minutes after they entered and attempted to warm themselves at the fire, the innkeeper brought a hot kidney pie, a steaming loaf of bread, a thick wheel of cheese, and placed them on the table beside mugs of ale.

When the innkeeper left, Louisa closed the door behind him. She glanced in the cloudy mirror and quickly looked away. She was dirty and disheveled, her habit waterlogged and filthy. He didn't look any better.

In the corner was the basin of warm water the innkeeper had left. After Louisa dabbed at her face and got much of the dirt off, he attempted to scrub his face and hands.

Finally she pulled off her boots and placed them by the fire and tried to smooth her hair.

"Your boots won't dry, you know. Not in the short time we'll be here."

"I know," she answered. "But it makes me feel better to do that. For a moment, part of me will be warm." She rested her bare feet on the hearth. He thought how scandalized the old Miss Prim would have been at Louisa's actions.

As they ate, Louisa asked what they would do once they arrived at the Home Office. "Do you believe Lasington's men will surround the city and not allow us in?"

"I can't imagine how they would do that. There are so many roads into London that such a plan would take thousands of men." He sliced a piece of bread and took a bite before continuing. "Were I Lasington, I'd place many of his men as patrols on the road and some surrounding the Home Office. That way, they could grab me before I entered."

"Wouldn't they be obvious to anyone in the street?"

"No, his spies will look like normal citizens and won't bother anyone but you or me." He leaned forward, trying to frighten Louisa into staying at the inn. "They would take us away very quietly, so no one would notice."

"I would shout and fight." She shoveled a large piece of kidney pie in her mouth.

"You'd not have a chance. They'd move so quickly and not have the slightest qualm about harming you to keep you quiet."

"They could not do that." Louisa picked up the last bite of the bread. "How will we get inside with all those men around?"

"I don't know. Right now, I am just hoping we get to London."

"How long will it take to get to London? Can we keep traveling in this rain?"

"With the rain slowing us down, I don't know. If we were able to travel at the usual rate of speed, I'd guess we are between two and three hours from London. In this weather, I worry that we won't get there today." He looked out the window at the dark sky. "The road has to be getting worse. I don't want to hurt the horses or endanger us."

"What will happen if we can't get our message to the Home Office immediately?" She looked up at him, her brow wrinkled.

"It means," William said slowly and without meeting her eyes, "England is in much greater peril." He looked out the window.

"And us?" she asked insistently, putting her hand on his arm until he turned to face her. "What about us?"

He put his hand over hers. "Louisa, if I could do this all over again, I would have left you at Longtrees. In fact, I would have told Cassie not to write you, that I'd work out something on my own. I would do anything not to have you involved in this."

"Well, we don't have that luxury now, William. All of that happened and there's nothing we can do except keep going."

He took her hand and held it before placing a kiss in the center of her palm.

Chapter Fifteen

The horses splashed through the downpour, making little headway against the billowing wind and muck of the saturated road. "I don't know how much longer we can travel!" William shouted.

They had warmed up at the little inn and their horses had eaten and been rubbed down. However, anxious to get back on the road, they'd left when a small area of blue sky appeared. Clouds had covered it only shortly after they began to ride again.

Frowning, he glanced back at Louisa who struggled to keep up with him.

Louisa didn't answer. What could she say? She knew William would keep going as long as possible, but when the road became impassable, what then?

He did not speak again but concentrated on the road.

Her world had shrunk to William's back a few feet in front of them, the smell of wet horse, the darkness, and interminable rain.

The storm consumed her thoughts. The pounding downpour and the wind swirling around them drowned out all other sounds. Would they hear the traitors if they rode up behind them? Louisa doubted it.

She worried she was pushing Bess too hard. With every jolt from the increasingly slippery and almost flooded road, she worried about Bess.

If any good came of this storm, it was that she didn't believe the spies were following them. They hadn't found their trail before, and she doubted these hirelings were dedicated enough to the French cause to put themselves through this kind of discomfort. She guessed most of them would far prefer a fire and a mug of ale to racketing around the countryside in this weather.

Then Bess slipped and almost fell. Louisa did fall, sliding off the back of the mare as the horse struggled to right herself.

"William!" she shouted as she picked herself up.

"Are you hurt?" he shouted, riding back toward her.

"No, the mud cushioned my fall, but Bess could have broken a leg. We dare not go further." Louisa gently picked up the horse's foreleg and felt it gingerly. "No, she's all right this time, but the roads are so bad our horses are going to hurt themselves and us."

William looked at the sky. She could tell in his

expression and the way he held his body that he didn't want to stop.

"Killing a horse or ourselves won't get us to London any faster."

He nodded. "Tomorrow it may be drier. We'll attempt it then." He looked around. "I think we may be a little past Ilford. As I remember, there is a small inn ahead." He helped Louisa back on Bess and they rode the short distance.

"I'll take the horses to the stable!" William shouted against the wind when no groom greeted them. "You go ahead and talk to the innkeeper."

Louisa hurried to the inn, delighted at the thought of something to eat and a warm place to sleep.

With a smile, the innkeep welcomed her inside.

"My husband and I would like a private parlor and two bedrooms."

"I'm sorry, my lady," the innkeep apologized. "We have only one bedroom left. With all the rain, you see, we have filled all the others. It's a small one, too, but it has a nice, soft, warm bed. We'll set a lovely fire."

"If it's all you have, we'll have to take it, gratefully. And a private parlor?"

"Well, we have one that another traveler has just left. If you don't mind waiting, we'll bring your meal."

"That would be most acceptable. We will want it for the rest of the day."

The innkeeper nodded. "Now, allow me to show you

the way." He took her to the parlor, opened the door, and bowed as he left her.

In the small room, Louisa attempted to dry her hair in the warmth of the fire, running her fingers through its tangles as she knelt on the hearth. She looked up to see William, who had stopped just inside the door to watch her.

"I know. It won't do any good, but I like to seem to be doing something to restore myself," Louisa said.

There was an expression of longing on his face that surprised Louisa and reminded her of earlier days. As he watched her, she could not break the contact between them, tenuous as it was. "William?"

He walked to where she stood and took a ringlet of her hair in his hand. "Like the darkness of midnight."

"And here's some nice spiced punch for you," the host said as he bustled in with a steaming bowl and two cups.

William dropped his hand and watched the host fill the cups and give one to Louisa.

"That will warm you up from that cold rain outside."

Louisa took a sip. It was hot and burned her tongue but its heat began to thaw her.

William moved to look out the window. "Dark as midnight out there, too, and it's barely afternoon."

In a few minutes, a young girl came in with a tray of boiled mutton and potatoes. She set plates and bowls on the table, but William continued to look out the window. When the servant left, he turned around and took the cup of punch Louisa held out to him.

"That does help." He sat and picked up a napkin.

After they had eaten, William again looked out the window, at the sheets of rain that beat against it. "Blast the wait," he said. "Here we stay, isolated in this inn while Lasington sits in London and pulls the strings."

He stood there for a few more minutes before he turned toward Louisa. "Are we sharing a room again?"

Louisa nodded as she chewed on a bit of mutton that threatened to break her teeth. When she finally swallowed it, she said, "The inn is full."

He nodded. "Why don't you ask the innkeeper to make a fire in the bedroom. Go up there and rest. I'll stay down here for a few hours."

The room was warm and the bed was soft. Louisa took off her wet clothing and hung it by the fire before she lay down, pulled a quilt over her and fell asleep to the soft sound of rain against her window.

She awoke to silence. Stumbling out of her bed, she went to the window to look out on the dark stable yard. The rain had stopped although the wind was still blowing.

Turning, she searched through the sodden bundle William had brought in and found her brush. She ran it through her hair then checked her reflection in the mirror: Riotous hair and eyes that looked enormous in her pale face. Well, there was nothing she could do about any of it now she thought as she pulled on the damp clothing.

"My lady," the innkeep said when she went to the door to the parlor, "I'll bring you a light supper when you are ready."

Louisa smiled at the innkeep. "Would you serve us in an hour? My husband may still be resting." She tiptoed into the near darkness of the room where snores echoed.

She allowed William to sleep awhile, and by the light of the fire she read a newspaper she found on the table. When his snores stopped, she moved next to the chair where he slept and said, "William, it's stopped raining."

"What?" William almost knocked her on the floor in his haste to get to the window. "Look at that. The wind should help dry the roads, if it doesn't bring more rain." He turned around. "We may reach London tomorrow."

"Only twenty-four hours late."

"Couldn't be helped. We'll get there and stop Lasington."

"Yes, William." And that would mean the end of her adventures. Oh, she hated the fear of the journey and the suspense of waiting and wondering, but she loved the thrill, the excitement, and yes, even the danger. What she hated most was that soon she would have to become the straitlaced Louisa again.

What made her saddest was the knowledge that reaching London would mean the end of her time with William.

She quickly turned away from him to poke at the embers in the fireplace. When they flared to life, she lit the candles.

The innkeep stood at the door with a tray. He entered and placed a loaf of bread and some cheese on the table with a tray. "I have a nice pot of hot tea to warm you and here's tasty pudding for after dinner." The innkeeper placed the dishes on the table as he named them.

"I know we'll both enjoy it." Louisa smiled at the innkeep. "And, could someone please awaken us at six tomorrow morning?"

"Of course, my lady." The innkeep bowed his way out of the parlor.

While they ate, they didn't speak. Even after he'd finished the last bite on his plate, they sat in silence for a few minutes before William asked, "Would you like to play cards? I found some on the table. Piquet?"

"I hope you don't play for chicken stakes."

"Of course not. However, Miss Prim, I'd think you would."

"Never! A penny a point."

"Ahh, quite daring."

They cleared the table and pulled it in front of the fire where Louisa shuffled the greasy cards.

The dinner had long since been removed and Louisa had asked for spiced tea which had almost disappeared by the time William counted out the coins to pay his debt. "Half a crown, Louisa. You're a regular Captain Sharp."

"I always fleeced the boys who came down from Oxford with my brothers." Louisa laughed. "You don't want to play Beggar Your Neighbor with me."

"I've been warned." He paused. "Why don't you go up to our chambers? I'd like to have an ale."

"You do not plan to spend the night down here, do you?"

"Why not? As I explained, I am attempting to guard your reputation."

"Oh, as if riding all day then stopping in a tavern would not ruin me, even if you did stay in the private parlor. Besides, it would look foolish, suspicious. No husband would spend the night in a private parlor unless he and his wife had just had a terrible fight."

She could tell he was contemplating that.

"And consider this: If the spies came by, there you'd be, sitting in the parlor waiting for them. Or I would be alone in our room where they could take off with me without your knowing."

"That is possible." He nodded. "We can probably arrange this comfortably and keep your virtue intact."

Louisa filled her cup again and took another sip of the warming beverage before she stood. "I'll go up first, to wash up and rest."

Louisa lay in bed, finishing the newspaper by the flickering light of the lamp. It was close to ten o'clock. In spite of her long nap, she was exhausted, but where was William? She'd been in bed for over an hour.

Finally, as she pondered, she realized she did know why he hadn't returned. He was being so very responsible that he thought she'd be asleep by the time he came up from the tap room. Thought he could sneak in without waking her, and spend the night on that lumpy old chair.

She looked around the tiny room. Again, she'd hung her clothes in front of the dying fire and wore her chemise to sleep in because she'd forgotten to pack a nightgown. In the corner stood the large chair where, she imagined, he planned to sleep.

She stood and looked out the window. She could hear the wind rattling the panes of glass and roaring around the building, but she didn't see any rain. Oh, please, let it stay dry tonight, she prayed.

But where was he? Why didn't the stupid, gallant rogue come to bed?

Perhaps the light showed under the door. Perhaps that was why he didn't come upstairs. She blew the lamp out, jumped into bed and pulled the covers up. After almost twenty minutes, she heard footfalls in the hallway and closed her eyes. The door opened just a little. He paused before he entered and shut it behind him. She could hear his quiet breathing and stayed silent. She could hear him as he placed his candle on the table next to the chair, then took off his boots, put them on the hearth, and removed his unmentionables which he arranged close to the fire with his coat.

"You won't leave tonight, will you?" Louisa whispered. "You won't ride out without me?"

"I have learned," he said, "that it doesn't do a bit of good. You just follow me." After a pause, he added, "Good night, Miss Prim."

When a tap came at the door, Louisa awoke and groggily answered, "Yes?"

"It's six. I'll leave a pitcher of warm water out here," said a maid. "Do you want your fire built up?"

"No, that's fine," William said.

Louisa looked over to see him dressed and looking out the window. "What's the weather like?"

"Clear and dry. It looks like a lovely day to foil the French." He turned back to her with a smile. "Your clothing is almost dry. Get dressed while I order us breakfast."

After she dressed, she looked out the window. The sun shone, the wind blew slightly, and the road looked dry. It was a beautiful morning.

It was time to go to London.

Chapter Sixteen

As if to make up for the terrible weather the day before, it was a lovely morning. Louisa could smell the dampness of wood and mud, although the latter might have come from her habit. She'd brushed it and brushed it but still the merino almost crackled as she walked. But that odor was almost concealed by the scent of flowers carried on a gentle breeze. The sun shone brilliantly, flickering through the thick leaves of trees that surrounded the yard. From the front of the inn, where she stayed to keep her boots from getting even more covered with mud, Louisa watched the groom bring the horses from the stable.

"The road looks much better, my lord," she heard the innkeeper tell William. "The trip should take less than two hours."

"Then let's go." William made a hand for Louisa and threw her on Bess. "Home Office, Whitehall," he said as he mounted Charger.

They rode in silence on roads much drier and safer, but here and there was a patch of mud or a puddle and the ruts were deep.

Every now and then, William glanced back at her. With his profile silhouetted against the bright morning, Louisa could see the grim set to his mouth but forbore mentioning it until the fifth time he turned and studied her.

"What worries you?" she asked. "Particularly?" As if she didn't know. The man was going to lecture her again, but she saw no way to avoid it unless she galloped off ahead of him.

When he slowed and moved next to Louisa, she could see the concern in his eyes as he looked at her.

"Well, in particular, you do. Even though you have the heart of Wellesley and the courage of a lion, I cannot stop worrying about what could happen to you."

"Oh, for heaven's sake, William. You must stop worrying."

He looked down at her as if he were filling his eyes and mind with her image. "Louisa, I want you to promise me one thing."

"William, I know what you're going to say."

"Louisa, when we get to Whitehall," he said in a somber voice, "you stay behind me. I'll go inside and get help. My friends will be there to take charge.

Everything will be over in no time at all. Just wait for me where you'll be safe."

She gazed up at him, attempting to convince him with an expression as sweet and innocent as possible. "Of course, William. Whatever you say."

"Blast it, Louisa, I know you. You're going to do something foolish, aren't you? Why can't you be content to sit and wait until it's all over? Until it's safe?"

"I will. I promise to stay out of danger if everything works out well, but I'm not going to be a mere onlooker if you need me."

They heard horses approaching from behind them, moving fast. William pulled Bess and Charger into the trees again as the horses raced past.

"It's they," Louisa stated. "I recognize one of the horses. They went right past us. Does that mean we're safe?"

"I don't know. We can only hope that they are leaving this section of the road unguarded." They moved from the trees. "Except . . ."

"Except what?"

"I think in a short distance, there is a junction where this road meets an important highway."

"And?"

"The riders could be going to that crossroads. They must realize they lost us in the storm and are covering some of the major roads on this side of London."

"We could turn around and try another way."

"No, that would take so long. Who knows which

ones are being watched and what Lasington could do in that amount of time? I think the best thing to do is for us to walk around the traitors."

"Walk around them? With the horses?"

William looked ahead at a small farm. "I'll see if I can find someone to help us."

Shortly, the farmer had joined them with instructions to ride Charger and lead Bess through the road block they could now see ahead and meet them on the other side.

"Tell them two men hired you to take the horses to the city," William said.

Walking around the traitors was far more difficult than finding the farmer and sending the horses ahead. After they climbed a stone fence to the north of the road, Louisa and William followed a path close to the highway but hidden from it by trees. It took only minutes to arrive at the intersecting road.

When they looked to the left, they saw the traitors were inspecting vehicles at the crossing, exactly as William had predicted. While they watched through thick bushes, the three men stopped a carriage and made the elderly passenger get out while they searched it.

"They'll see us when we cross," Louisa said. She looked to the right but the road stretched out straight with nothing to impede the view of the men guarding the crossing.

"We'll think of something."

They considered the situation for a minute before

William said. "I'll get close to them and throw some stones toward the waiting horses. After the animals start moving around and making noise, you run across the road. When you get across, you do the same for me."

With no better idea, Louisa agreed. She waited in the woods for almost five minutes before she heard the commotion with the horses. When she did, she darted over to the other side of the road without any of the spies seeing her.

That was easy. She walked along the edge of the forest and she kept herself hidden from the traitors by a narrow screen of trees until she was almost near enough to pick up and throw the stones.

"Hey!" shouted one of the men at the crossing. "What's that? Do you hear someone in the trees?"

Louisa stood still, trying to hide herself behind a very thin oak as a man approached the edge of the woods.

"Howard, you come with me. I think someone's hiding in the trees. Maybe one of the people we're looking for."

The men started into the forest. Where could she hide? Louisa looked around her. The only possibility she saw was a thicket. Throwing herself on the ground, she wiggled through a bush with thorns. The sharp spikes slashed her skin. Grateful to be so slender, Louisa squirmed as far as she could and pulled her feet in after her but the area was so little she didn't fit completely. Her toes probably showed outside the thicket.

She held her breath, trying to hear where the men were, frustrated that she could do nothing to cover her feet and frightened that they would see them. As she lay there, she became aware of the pain of her scratches as blood dripped from her cheek and across her nose.

Louisa also realized she shared the space with other creatures. Something crawled over her. No, that was wrong. Many things crawled over her. Perhaps several types of insects marched across her ankles and neck. She shuddered and hoped they didn't bite. On top of that, the ground was wet and cold. She was chilled and covered with even more mud.

"Ben, there's no one here. You're always imagining things."

The voice came from just above the thicket, directly over her head. If there had been room, Louisa would have jumped in surprise but she couldn't move, so stuck in the branches and thorns was she.

"Must've heard a deer."

"All right," said the man she guessed was Ben. "Let's go back to the road, but I'm going to keep an ear cocked in this direction."

Louisa heard the two men trudge back to the road. After a few minutes of silence, she attempted to back out of the thicket but couldn't move. She most certainly could not move silently. Every time she tried, the leaves rustled and the thorns dug more deeply into her flesh.

Her hands were stuck above her head because she'd

used them to burrow into the thicket. Now they were embraced so tightly by the prickly brush that they couldn't move either. Nor could she push herself out with her elbows. When she attempted to dig them into the mud, they slid and left her no purchase.

Every time she tried to wiggle out, the thorns tore her skirt and scratched her legs, and the leaves rustled.

I'm going to die here. William won't be able to find me. I'll starve. Crawly creatures will build nests in my hair, and little woodland animals will nibble on my toes.

Exhausted and maudlin for a moment, she envisioned her funeral. Her entire family would be in attendance to talk about what a wonderful sister and aunt she was. Would William be there? Would he talk about what a courageous woman she was and how she helped to save their beloved isle? Even Prinny—the Regent, the Prince of Wales—might be there to give a tribute to her as a heroine who'd given her life for her country.

Oh, for goodness sake, Louisa. She didn't want Prinny to speak at her funeral. No, not at all. She really didn't want a funeral. She was made of much stronger stuff. She was, after all, a flower of British womanhood, and a flower of British womanhood did not wither up and die because she had been captured by a thicket.

With that thought, she pulled with her feet again. She still didn't move and her ankle scraped painfully against the prickly spikes.

"Blast it," she muttered.

"Louisa?" William's whisper came from the same place the men had stood only minutes earlier. "Where are you?"

"Down here, stuck in the bush."

He kneeled down and looked into her face. "Come out. We need to get going."

"I would love to, but I *cannot* get out. If I could, I'd have met you long ago. I'm afraid you're going to have to leave me here or dig up the bush and carry the whole thing to London."

She could tell he was having trouble not laughing. She didn't find it funny, but then there were bugs crawling all over her.

Louisa could hear him walk around the bush, probably contemplating her plight. Then he returned to where her feet stuck out, grasped her ankles and pulled her straight backward. It was noisy, so he waited for another vehicle to approach before he continued.

Little by little, she could feel herself being extracted from the prickly prison. She bit her lip against the pain, but when her face skimmed across the wet leaves and she was out, she was filled with delight. Mud covered her from head to toe, which she *did* mind, but there was little she could do about that.

"Come on," he whispered. "We've got to run."

"Howard, d'you hear anything in the woods?" Ben's voice came from the road. Both Louisa and William froze.

"Nothing, but keep listening."

When William gave Louisa his hand, she stood as quietly as she could. They started to walk but were so close to the road they feared they would make too much noise as they pushed through more thick brush.

As a branch broke under William's boot, Ben shouted. Both Louisa and he stood still until they heard a wagon approach. When the traitors waved the wagon through, Louisa and William moved with its noise but stopped when the sounds no longer covered the crackling of branches.

This went on for the next thirty minutes: They traveled short distances when the sound of a vehicle masked the rustling they made, then held still until another rig arrived. When they were finally out of the spies' earshot, William looked down at Louisa, lips trembling with the effort of not laughing.

"Oh, go ahead and laugh, if you must. But first, tell me how in the world you got across."

"When the two men disappeared into the woods, I was afraid they were going to find you. While the third man searched a cart, I ran to this side."

He brushed something off her cheek. She didn't want to know what it was.

"I won't ask what happened to you," he said. "It's obvious. Did anything bite you?"

"I don't think these insects were the biting kind. Most were the crawling-all-over kind. Some of them still are."

William took her hand and pulled her along the forest trail until they found their horses. After he and Louisa jumped on Charger and Bess, William tossed a coin to the farmer.

Louisa tried to clean up but decided there really was no need. Her gown was ruined. As well as mud, there were other stains—she shuddered to contemplate their origin—which would never come out. Wet leaves still clung to her dress and body.

"I think I have a thorn in my chin. Can you see it?"

William turned back to inspect her smudged face. "Ahh, yes, you do. I think I can grab the end." He drew it out. "Let me clean you up a little."

He used his handkerchief to rub the larger patches of dirt from her face then sniffed the air surrounding Louisa. "You are incredibly dirty. Not that I don't find the odor of decayed plants and mud appealing, but you do need a bath. I am embarrassed to be traveling with such an odiferous hoyden."

She glared at him but could not disagree.

Chapter Seventeen

As they turned onto Cheapside almost two hours later, they passed St. Paul's, Fleet Street, and the Temple. The nearer they got to the Strand and Whitehall, the more nervous she became. What would they find there? Who would they find there?

And the question she didn't want to consider—*would* they get there?—refused to stop haunting her mind.

The rest of the ride—such a short trip!—took forever and yet not long enough. As they rode, Louisa kept looking for Lasington's men.

When they stopped across the street from the Home Office, Louisa and William searched the faces of people in the street.

"Those men over there." Louisa pointed inconspicuously. "Near the church. I recognize them. Especially the bald man."

William nodded. "They're too far away to reach me by the time I enter the building. There must be more spies closer to the entrance."

"Maybe that group." Louisa studied several well-dressed men who stood by the columns at the entrance to the building.

"Possibly."

"How do we get inside?"

"Louisa, there is no 'we' in this situation." He counted eight men, but there could be more. How would he get past eight of them? "My friends are inside. If I can get close . . ."

While he continued to scrutinize the building, the placement of the men, and tried to come up with a plan, he said, "Louisa, you *will* stay here." Then he looked at Bess, but Louisa was no longer on the mare. No, she was standing beside Bess, and if he was any judge, she was preparing to run across the street. Idiot, heroic little idiot.

She took a deep breath and started to run. As she took off, his heart rose to his throat. He knew in a flash that if anything happened to her, he'd never forgive himself. *Oh, Lord, please don't let her be hurt. If you promise to keep her safe, I'll marry her, even if she'll probably drive me crazy.*

With a leaping dismount, he grabbed Louisa after

she had run only five or six paces, just as she had opened her mouth and yelled, "I'm the one—"

He put his hand over her lips to keep her quiet.

"Woodstone?" a woman said. He nodded at the startled Duchess of Worth like a perfect gentleman. He was sure the gossip that he'd been struggling with a woman of a certain kind—although he was sure women of *that* kind would never be as dirty and smelly as Louisa—would be talked about in every parlor and salon in London in a few hours. Thank goodness the duchess hadn't recognized Louisa in her present state and with his hand over her mouth.

After looking across the street to see if any of the men had noticed them, he pulled Louisa behind a column. "What the blazes were you doing?"

"I was drawing their attention so you could get into the building." She explained as if he were exceptionally slow in his understanding. "I was going to say, 'I'm the one Lasington is looking for' because, otherwise, how would they know that is who I am? They would think I was a filthy crazy lady running toward them unless they recognized me. That would be doubtful so I decided to identify myself.

"Now, if you will just let me go." She glanced down at her wrists which he held in his hand and she could not loosen. "If you will just let me go, I will finish the distraction while you go in and get your friends."

"Louisa," he said with a shake of his head. "Don't

you understand how dangerous this is? Don't you know what those men would have done to you if they knew who you were?"

"Yes."

"Do you realize it would *not* take eight men to take care of a woman? That there would be several left to kill me?"

"Of course I realized that. I thought you could take care of the others."

He couldn't help but laugh. "You have much more confidence in me than I do. Even I wouldn't attempt to get past four or five men with weapons. And what happened to the 'We are partners' idea that you talked about all the time? Have you forgotten we're in this together?"

"I didn't think."

"On top of that, don't you know how much I would suffer if those men harmed you?"

"Oh? You would?" She thought for a moment. "In all the excitement, I hadn't considered that either."

"I would prefer for you to stay alive until we can discuss exactly that. Now, we're going to have to come up with another plan, together."

"We could sneak around behind people to get closer," she suggested but he shook his head. No one would let her too close to them.

"I could draw them off while you slip in," William said.

"How would a stinky, dirty person like me get into

the ministry and see anyone important? And what would happen to you while I was going inside?"

They studied the street and the building in silence.

"Is there another entrance?" she asked. "In the back? Through one of the buildings on the side?"

"There is an exit in the back, but I don't have a key. If there is an entrance through the other buildings, well"—he shrugged—"they haven't told me about it."

As a carriage passed, Louisa said, "Perhaps we could hire a vehicle to take us closer and we could rush in." Then she eyed the men standing close to the doors and shook her head. "No, we'd never make it."

Silently, they thought and planned and plotted. After a few minutes, Bess nudged Louisa on the shoulder. Unconsciously, she scratched the mare's nose before shoving her away, but Bess kept nudging her.

"I know you're hungry, Bess, but we have to do this first."

"Too bad we can't take the horses," William said. "As hungry as they are, if there was food inside, no one could stop them."

They looked at each other and said, in unison, "Of course. The horses."

The idea turned out to be astonishingly simple: They would mount the horses and ride them in through the front doors, hoping the animals would not be afraid to enter and that the men guarding the building wouldn't attempt to stop the galloping steeds.

"Not much of a plan," Louisa said.

"But the best we have. You go first. Charger will not allow anyone to get to me, but you might get through when they are too surprised to respond."

They gathered the reins tightly in their hands and trotted to the end of the street, then galloped back, making a fast, angled turn toward the ministry. With the speed they had gathered, even the unwillingness of the horses to enter the building didn't hurt because the thugs scattered when they saw Bess coming toward them. Once in and with no time to spare, they handed the reins to a startled guard and ran across the marble lobby and up the stairs.

William looked over his shoulder as he rounded the first landing. There was no one behind him although he heard running footsteps entering the building. Louisa had lifted her skirt and sprinted ahead of him until he overtook her and led her to Fothergill's office. He hoped Fothergill and one of the others would be there as he'd instructed them.

Once on the first floor, he passed Lasington's office. The sound of movement came from inside the traitor's office which startled William. Certainly he wasn't still here? But, why not? With his men guarding the doors and surrounding the building, Lasington clearly felt confident using the Home Office as the center of his operations.

William wanted to go into the office and thrash the man for putting Louisa and the baby in danger. Although that would give him great personal pleasure, he had to pass on the identity of the spy and the location of little Beatrice first.

Inside the central office area, he felt safe. The guard looked at him in momentary surprise at the state of his apparel but said, "Good day, my lord."

"Smythe, get some more men to the front door and to these offices," William said calmly and forcefully. "I fear there may be some spies coming."

The guard moved to do William's bidding but not before his mouth fell open when he saw Louisa.

With bark in her hair, her face scratched, disreputable riding habit, and an unpleasant odor surrounding her, no wonder the guard was puzzled.

William turned to another guard and said, "Go get Godwell and Bradenton and tell them I need to talk to them in Fothergill's office." He took Louisa's hand and dragged her behind him.

"I can walk on my own," she protested, but he didn't let go of her.

Fothergill was in his office, leaning back in the chair with his feet on the desk, asleep.

"Wake up!" William pulled Louisa inside, slammed the office door and pounded on the desk.

Fothergill leaped from his chair and stared at William. "You look terrible. Where have you been?" he asked with a yawn.

Then he sniffed the air. "What's that odor?" Finally he saw Louisa. "Lady Louisa, how lovely to see you. Won't you have a seat."

And, as politely as if she was eating crumpets for tea instead of fleeing from spies, Louisa sat and said, "Thank you."

Godwell appeared at the door. "What the . . . is that Woodstone? Where have you been? You're a little unkempt." He studied Louisa and said, "Good day, Lady Louisa. How lovely to see you."

Bradenton followed Godwell and said, "I say, Woodstone . . ."

"Give me your coat, Fothergill, and listen to what I have to tell you." Before he could say more, Smythe hurried in.

"Everything is under control, my lord," Smythe said. "When the other guards and I got to the front door, a number of men were riding off, but we've posted more guards at the entrances."

"Put a guard around Lasington's office. Do not let him know you are there, Smythe, but if he tries to leave do not let him. Keep him there no matter what you have to do."

"Yes, my lord." Smythe left the office.

"We don't have much time. I don't want Lasington to leave before I talk to him." William took off his coat and pulled the clean one over his stained shirt. "Fothergill, write this down as I talk so we can pass it on."

William quickly sketched the events of the past few days and Louisa added a few points. When they finished the story, the three men understood the situation although they could not believe Lasington had aided the French. They also knew where the baby was and how to get her back.

"I have one more thing I have to do, Louisa." He turned to her and took her hand. "You must stay here. In order for me to get Lasington to confess, I'll need to tell him that his men have you. Please stay here with Bradenton."

He knew she hated to be left out, but she agreed. After telling another guard to take the notes Fothergill had written to Robert Ryder, the Secretary of State for the Home Office, the men went down the hall to Lasington's office.

"Stay out here," William said as he knocked. "Come inside only if I ask you to."

"Who is it?" came Lasington's deep voice from the office.

Without answering, William entered. He wanted to see the expression on Lasington's face and wasn't disappointed. The spy sat behind his desk and had been making notes.

Before the marquis could hide his shock, William pounced. "Weren't expecting me, were you, Lasington? You thought your men would kill me before I could pass on any information."

"I have no idea what you mean." Lasington calmly turned the paper over and assumed his usual bored appearance.

"Don't dissemble, Lasington. We know who you are."

The marquis didn't answer.

"As you see, your men didn't succeed." William moved closer to the desk. "I have conveyed the details about your activities to Ryder. You will be tried as a spy."

"Which is not a bad epitaph when one dies for what one believes."

"You believe in the French cause?" William stared down at Lasington before seating himself. "You didn't do this for money?"

"What need do I have for money? Our family has enough for me to live more than comfortably. I spied for principle." He laughed at the fury in William's expression. "Odd isn't it? Patriotic British nobleman, raised in the bosom of the finest our country has to offer."

"Why? How could you betray your country?"

"France is my country. There I see the discipline, the structure Napoleon has given his empire—my empire! Here we have the choice of a dotty old king or a frivolous regent who never saw a palace that didn't need a new turret. He'll drive the country into debt in no time. Any wonder I prefer the Bonaparte?"

"But Lasington, how could you decide to kill a baby?"

"Now I admit I wasn't happy about doing that. I don't believe I would have actually killed it. Probably would have used it for leverage, then, after we learned what we needed from your man, we would've killed the spy and given the baby to a fine French family to raise correctly. So, you see, I am not as black as you would paint me." He flashed a charming smile at William.

"Yes you are, Lasington." William returned the smile with a snarl. "Not only have you betrayed your country, but your men have taken Lady Louisa."

"That prim woman? Why would I care? In the balance, will her life make any difference when compared with my cause?"

"In the balance, her life means a great deal. You see, she is the woman I plan to marry."

"Well, to you she was important, but you will find another," Lasington said coolly. "After all, one is much like another."

William stood, grabbed the marquis by the shoulders and dragged him to his feet. "For God's sake, man, do something decent. You said you spied for your beliefs. You wouldn't have killed the baby. Don't go to the gallows with the death of a woman on your soul. Tell me where to find her."

"You beg? Woodstone, I'm amazed. What will you trade me for her?" Lasington pulled away as he studied William's features. "What should I ask for?"

"Anything."

"Will you allow me to escape?"

He paused as if struggling with his conscience. "If you tell me where she is, I will allow you to leave this office unhindered."

"You will make no attempt to seize me or stop me?" Lasington again attempted to read William's expression.

"I will make no attempt to seize you. I will stay here."

"You must love her very much to trade her for a spy."

"She is a very unusual woman who would not ask that of me." William forced himself not to look toward the door.

"You must understand I'm not certain where she is. They might have taken her to Green's farms in Surrey."

"But you're not sure?"

"No, I wasn't interested. My part is finished if I can't find the baby. Would you trade the baby for her?" When William glowered, Lasington said, "No, I didn't think so but thought I'd try. All in all, my freedom is enough."

"Where is this farm?"

"Go south, past Epsom." He smiled up at William. "Now, am I free to go?"

"Almost." William sat on the desk and studied Lasington. "What about Etienne D'Estange? How can we find him?"

Lasington shrugged. "I know absolutely nothing about the man. I met with him occasionally. He gave me money to hire men, even rode with us a few times, but I could never trace him."

William took a step toward Lasington.

"I swear, that's all I know about him. I don't even know if he's French. The man could assume any accent."

"What does he look like?"

"Thin, medium height, light hair. Nothing unusual about him." Impatient, Lasington drummed his fingers on the desk.

When William sat down again, the marquis opened his drawer, and picked up a stack of money.

"I didn't plan this well." Lasington stuffed the bills in a small bag. "I should have left much earlier but thought there was no chance you would get through."

William watched the marquis' preparations with feigned composure.

Snapping the bag shut, Lasington took a dueling pistol from a drawer and turned it toward William.

"I assume this means you are not going to take me up on my offer to leave unimpeded?"

"Certainly, Woodstone, you cannot think I'd believe you would allow me to walk out of my office and the Home Office to disappear." Lasington shook his head. "You must think I'm a fool not to know you are a man of honor, a man who loves his country, a man who would never allow his emotion to sway him from his duty. A man who would never allow a spy to escape."

William stayed in the chair as Lasington waved the pistol.

"Who do you have waiting for me out there?" Lasington asked as he moved around the desk, carefully staying away from William.

"I came alone." William turned in his chair to watch the spy.

"Woodstone, Woodstone." Lasington shook his head.

"You know me better than that." Brandishing the pistol, he took a step toward William. "How many men are outside this door?" He moved toward the window and looked out. "And down there? How many men do you have?"

"I won't tell you, Lasington. Shoot me if you must, but I will not tell you anything."

The marquis gazed out the window again. "It's only one story from here to the street." He considered for a moment. "Which do you think would be better? To jump from the window and hope for a soft landing or to leave through the door and run into whomever you have waiting for me out there?"

Lasington turned away from the window and walked toward William. "Neither of those appeal to me," he said. "My plan is that you, Woodstone, are going to lead me out of here."

William lounged back in the chair. "How are you going to make me do that, Lasington? You can't force me to stand. If you pull me to my feet, you're going to have to move the pistol out of the way which may give me the opening I need to capture you. Of course, you could always kill me because I refuse to get up, but then you have nothing to bargain with, do you?" He yawned. "It's up to you, Lasington."

What in the world was going on in there?

Louisa could hear the voices inside, low and calm. Next to her stood Fothergill who kept whispering that

William would want her to return to the office. Only a few feet from her, Godwell and Bradenton paced in the hallway. A guard stood on each side of the door, and more were scattered by the staircase and in the corridor.

How could William think she would stay in safety when he was in danger? Certainly, he knew her well enough to know she had to be close to him. Louisa leaned against the wall, her ear only inches from the door.

There was, of course, no way she could help. She had no weapon and Lasington was far stronger than she.

The minutes dragged by. Once she heard a drawer slam. Then Lasington's voice came closer to the door before getting softer as he moved away.

From the office came the sound of a shot. Startled, Louisa jumped. Before she could start back toward the door, Fothergill dragged her away. She watched Godwell and Bradenton rush into the office and realized Fothergill needed to go with them, to help William.

"Go on," Louisa said. "I'll stay." At Fothergill's questioning look, she said, "I promise." Hearing the sound of fighting, she ran to stand by one of the guards by the staircase.

Oddly, after Fothergill entered the room, a man burst through the door. In only seconds, Lasington ran across the hall, grasped Louisa by the arm and put his other arm across her neck.

"I believe I have the upper hand," he said as William

raced out of the office and stopped when he saw the spy holding Louisa.

"William, you're bleeding." Louisa struggled to get away when she saw the blood running down his arm, but Lasington held her easily.

"It's not that serious, Lady Louisa," Lasington said. "He was trying to take my gun so I shot him, but the ball only hit him in the arm."

She didn't care where William was wounded. She just wanted to go to him.

William stopped a few feet from Louisa while Fothergill and Bradenton moved to each side of Lasington.

"Don't kill her," William said. "If you harm her, you'll be dead before you can move."

"Gentlemen, I am a dead man already. The only positive outcome of the situation would be for me to take someone with me."

"Take me!" William shouted. "You have nothing to gain by hurting a woman." He put his hand on the bleeding arm in an effort to staunch the bleeding.

"Ahh, but I do." Lasington tightened his arm around her neck. "I believe this will hurt you very much, Woodstone. That's enough for me now."

She watched William's eyes and thought she'd never seen such pain and fury in anyone's expression. Feeling Lasington's grasp loosen a little as he savored William's reaction, she threw her elbow back and hit Lasington in the ribs. As his arm moved a few inches from her neck in reaction to the blow, Louisa ducked and wrenched her body away from Lasington.

Then she hurled herself toward William, being careful not to touch the bleeding arm, and immediately burst into tears.

How mortifying.

"Louisa, it's fine." William's quiet voice pierced the fog of anger and panic. He held her against him and whispered softly to her. "Louisa, you're fine. The guards have put Lasington in chains. He won't hurt you."

Louisa peered over William's shoulder to see the guards pushing Lasington down the steps. Fothergill and Godwell stood between her and the traitor, who was screaming in French.

She nestled back against William because she felt warm and safe there. He ran his hand down her hair, loving and comforting her. When she finally calmed, he leaned back to look down at her.

"Louisa, why can't you ever stay where I put you?"

She didn't answer because, after all, he knew very well why she'd left the security of the office.

"I have never been so frightened." He pulled her back into his arms. "Louisa, I was afraid he was going to kill you. I couldn't have dealt with that." He paused to hold her close and breathe softly into her hair. "Louisa, I love you."

With his words and touch, the nightmare was over. She looked up at William with all the love that filled her. "I love you, too, William."

Louisa was jolted out of the lovely moment when Fothergill cleared his throat. William moved away, keeping her hand in his.

"Louisa, will you please do what I ask you to do this one time?"

She watched him suspiciously.

"Fothergill, I need you to smuggle Lady Louisa out the back door so no one will see her." At Fothergill's nod, William looked back at Louisa. "Which of your brothers or sisters is in town?"

"I believe Frederick is."

"Fothergill will take you to Frederick's house. He'll return you to your family to become a prim and proper woman again."

She looked down at her torn and stained dress and scratched boots and knew her face was covered with freckles. "I don't believe that is possible immediately."

"I will call on you as soon as possible, although with this arm, that may not be until tomorrow." He scowled down at her. "I warn you, Louisa. This time when I ask you to marry me, I will not allow you to turn me down."

"I would never consider that, William."

After dropping a kiss on her forehead, William said, "Don't try to fool me that you will ever be a docile wife, Louisa, because I know that is exactly what you will never be."

"Then why do you wish to marry me?"

"Because, Louisa, you are my heart." His voice

became low and sincere. "Because you are my heart, and I cannot live without you."

A smile lit her eyes and entire face and she could feel happiness well up inside her. "Well, if that's the case, of course I'll marry you."

And she gave him a kiss which was not at all prim.